Spring City Terror 1903

Sean Michael Malone

www.ten16press.com - Waukesha, WI

For information, please contact:

www.ten16press.com
Waukesha, WI

Edited by Christine Woods
Cover design by Teresa Carlson

For Linda,

My mother, first teacher, uncompromising guide,
and source of unending courage.

Fountain Spring House postcard, 1873

Preface

One way of understanding the "limits" of our daily lives is observing the physical space we interact with as we travel from work, to home, to leisure. I'm referring to what we can observe directly with our senses and the various news and information available to us from other places across the region, globe, or more recently, the cosmos. I'll extend this description to metaphor as our *fence* of perception and reality—what can be called the mundane, or rather, the natural world. Most will report that they have only encountered the mundane within their own fence, unless in cases where someone is convinced that they have directly witnessed a miracle or supernatural event. For the majority, while they can't assume that everything outside of their fence must also be mundane, they can, in good reason, say that it is almost certainly so, for the sake of simplicity. We have increasingly good cause to take this position in an internet-driven world of practically instant communication and increased scientific innovations. This is no fault of our own. It's not that we can actively seek other-worldly experiences even if we wanted to—apart from convictions held in religious belief or participation in fantasy-inspired media.

Yet there is something seductive and exciting in the idea that there are exceptions and breaks with the mundane, obscure and difficult as they may be to find. At the very least, it is pleasing to digest it in a way that seems rooted in daily experience but portrayed with just the right turn of fate or curious clue that leads to that daydreaming sense of a wondrous encounter. Many of us have imagined or dreamed of such a situation, sometimes even routinely. On the other hand, I'll cautiously posit that most people can and do find perfect contentment with a mundane existence (again, using the definition as it pertains to what is observable and a physical reality). That's not to say they are unimaginative or remotely idle as the term otherwise may indicate. Quite the opposite, in fact—they irrigate it with leisure activities, hobbies, and passions. There's certainly nothing wrong with finding wonder, beauty, and satisfaction in the natural world. It is those very traits, in fact, which make forays into mystery, fantasy, and strange reality meaningful—it is easier and more engaging to identify things outside of our defined boundaries. These forays offer a unique excavation to offer further insight into life itself, that stupendous and brief experience that defies our expectations in the most unexpected of ways.

The primary inspiration for this novel is the horror master H.P. Lovecraft, who presented a dark take on cosmic entities who shape the unseen. My understanding of Lovecraft's genius revolves around two concepts. The first is that he introduced a grand reservoir of impossibly remote and esoteric, arcane and blasphemous, uncaring and yet sinister intergalactic deities. He presented them through a tremendous outpouring of his imagination, rooted in nineteenth-century authors who touched on similar themes, evoked cultural legends, or reinvented myths. The second is that his stories predominantly feature ordinary yet thoughtful protagonists, supporting characters, and settings that are mundane but progressively revealed to be fantastic, connected, and horrific. These are very appealing elements of his genre; there is a sense of relation to his characters in discovering the eldritch and supernatural just around the corner in otherwise commonplace settings. The effectiveness of this escalating horror and the vividness of his descriptions of now popular entities such as Cthulhu established the considerable horror subculture of *weird fiction* and authors following his tradition. He was not the very first of this group, but he ultimately defined it.

One other name I'd like to mention is August Derleth. Where Lovecraft was the progenitor and imaginative foundation of what is now often referenced as the *Cthulhu Mythos*, Derleth was the compiler and organizer of these ideas that generated wider visibility. His role as publisher for most of Lovecraft's stories often overshadows his own writings. Derleth's own pursuits are controversial in certain perceptions; some argue he fundamentally altered the mysterious and unrestricted nature of Lovecraft's "Great Old Ones" in his broad categorizations and creative decisions. It is not the purpose of this introduction to assess the efficacy of Derleth's methods. Rather, it is to highlight that where Lovecraft hinted at or demonstrated the coexistence of these entities with some example, Derleth expanded and cemented the stories of Lovecraft and successive authors together in a wider universe. He is also appropriately credited with exponentially increasing the visibility of Lovecraft's works and popularizing this style.

While Derleth's own efforts and additions to the pantheon of cosmic entities bear his own signature, he also shares a connection to the following story as a Wisconsinite. Derleth was born and died in Sauk City, Wisconsin, and was a prolific writer of topics rooted in Wisconsin's geography and culture. He chose his native state as the setting for selections of his weird fiction and other stories, and he served as one inspiration for the following novel in that capacity. Furthermore, Derleth exemplifies the successors of Lovecraft in two ways. He could not escape from deriving in some way from the model set before him, and therefore he incorporated and adapted to it. This is a process that all authors undergo by some degree of course. They do not inhabit separate vacuums; it is always best to be cognizant of where we get our inspiration and acknowledge and celebrate these connections. Secondly, while Lovecraft infused his stories with the flavor of his native Massachusetts and other areas of New England, Derleth subsequently turned to the prairie land and "Driftless Area" of Wisconsin for his main saga.

When attempting to bridge the mundane and supernatural, Lovecraft and Derleth examined their own communities and stomping grounds. Local knowledge informs authors of names, dates, and places to supply the framework of an authentic setting and the evaporating or shifting pools of folklore. With these tools, authors are better-equipped to know which pockets of space on a map may best harbor portals to different planes of existence, enclaves of savage creatures, or collections where arcane manuscripts may be housed, much like Lovecraft's invented city of Arkham. The following is a story that I offer: one that is my own, but also simultaneously floating in that impalpable, cosmic mere of stories, casting ripples that impact the outer boundaries of our own maelstroms of the strange.

Prologue: The Hoaxer's Journey

Eugene Shepard was a hoaxer: full-time and professional. Although judging strictly off of his appearance as of late, one would guess it was not a lucrative venture. His usual outfit was brown or dark faded slacks with a matching vest and jacket, and he was fond of wearing a gray bowler hat, as he was this evening. His mustache had a natural droop to it, which regrettably mirrored his present countenance.

Eugene's "main" professions had varied, although none of them grasped him with that same passion compared to his primary interest of myth-weaving. He had reinvented the mythical *Hodag*, an absurd, ferocious critter that looked something like a hulking and oversized dog, or perhaps an undersized bull. Its hairless flesh was leathery, and it boasted a pair of horns. That's how his photograph displayed the beast, at least. In fact, this creature is now humorously associated with the pride of Rhinelander Wisconsin, but Eugene would never know this. The excitement from that exhibited photo of 1893 was drying up as it had aged one decade. Eugene needed a lead. Indeed, the art of the hoax is that you can never rely on one for too long, and a fresh act or presentation is needed to maintain the practice.

The dividends that the Hodag had provided Eugene were almost completely exhausted. Eugene stayed mobile, at least within his state, and that in and of itself cost money. He was also becoming progressively aware that he was growing old during the frequent and recurring dampness of the Wisconsin climate. The hoaxing practice did not merit many friends; indeed, it usually only spawned two types: part-time associates and long-term, bitter enemies. Eugene relied on the good-nature of his typically Midwestern audience to understand that entertainment, not swindling, was his primary craft. A proper hoax did not sow resentment but a contagious spark of conviviality in being privy to the truth, like being "in" on a good joke and enjoying its reception on a new audience. This environment fostered the feeling of being an insider, allowing deceptions to be enjoyed for their absurdness. Eugene pulled up the collar of his jacket to shelter his reddened neck as a chill wind assailed him. He was looking for new inspiration, although he had been brought somewhere rather uncomfortable in search of it.

The name of Eugene's present guide was a Mr. Thomas Moss. Moss was a man of mystery, with unkempt, shaggy hair and a thin beard. Eugene doubted that Moss, like himself, had a proper profession, making the two a likely pair. Eugene had once spied Moss looking at a gold-plated pocket watch, but Moss seemed to be very careful about ever taking it out and likely was unaware of being noticed. About a week ago, Eugene had first encountered the man at one of the more humble drinking establishments in Waukesha,

Wisconsin. The two had exchanged introductions amidst drifting smoke and cheap drink, and Eugene probed him as a possible information source. Moss was familiar with Shepard's notoriety but also dismissive. "That was a neat little joke you did," Moss began in his slow, thick voice, "but you really shouldn't fool folks like that. Not when there are real legends if you know where to find them. Dangerous ones at that, but fascinating." That had piqued Eugene's interest, and the resulting week had consisted of planning this expedition, meeting Moss at his odd hours of availability.

"You know, there's a lot of parts of Wisconsin that are about as obscure as frontier land out West," Moss continued. "I reckon the cartographers have mucked up some of the distance between the rivers south of the La Crosse. There's a lot more of the rough, untamed country than most people think. At any rate, Haunchyville is a real place, if you can pardon the vulgar name."

"You're not a fan of the name?" Eugene asked, amused, already trying to muster a better marketing term.

"Well, it's not its proper name, for one. Its real name is ancient and forgotten, although I've heard a few proposals that sound much nearer the mark than Haunchyville. Kahuxult, Chuhuyah, Xukattneh, Pytuh-"

"You've made your point," Eugene interrupted, unsure of whether Moss was inventing these names on the spot or if he was actually referencing some impossibly obscure knowledge from Lord knows where. "Now what exactly is—well, since I don't have a substitute name available—Haunchyville? An old indigenous ruin? Perhaps an incomplete or abandoned farmstead that time has rendered with endearing, peculiar features for the eye?"

"It's a damned village of little people," Moss said with a bit of a growl in his throat. "No, not those suffering from dwarfism, if that's what they're calling it these days. No sir, they have an encampment! It's a living, real fantasy in our own backyard! Depending on who you ask, you'll get a different location. But I know where it really is."

One thing that Eugene had decided early on about Moss was that he was not entirely present in his mental capacities. This did not present a substantial problem, however, and could be an advantage in Eugene fully assuming any benefits from what was at this alleged site. Eugene's thoughts returned to his present situation away from the hearth of the tavern. Unfortunately, finding a suitable location to pass as the site was proving difficult and time-consuming. Eventually, Moss agreed to lead Eugene to the fabled location.

The October day was getting on as the sunlight gradually waned. The pair had left around ten that morning after a delayed rendezvous, a full hour later than Eugene had desired. They generally followed the direction of the Fox River as it ran to the southwest. Moss had them meander further south, carefully noting property lines and landmarks known only to him, and then proceeding with a burst of enthusiasm. Eugene had become footsore and miserable. Whenever Moss's pace slackened, or the man looked lost, Eugene paused to inspect the soles of his shoes, scraping off the crushed crabapples and wet leaves. The pattern would always resume with wandering around some thickets and patches of trees, with Moss shaking his head and then muttering, "No, this isn't right." At least five hours had passed, in addition to their picnic lunch, without encountering another soul. Eugene found that odd for such a serviceable fall day, but Moss's claims were validated that people seldom happened upon the place or avoided doing so. Eugene had a general impression (but not a confident one) that they had meandered a few miles Southwest of Waukesha.

"Damn it Tom, I think I've had just about enough of this folly!"

"We're just about there, Mr. Shepard. I've already told you, it's only possible to find under the right conditions. It's some craft of the location; it's protected, enchanted to look like the same stretch of land you've already been on."

Eugene was angry at how convenient Moss's explanations were until he tripped forward over a large root that he had not seen. He thudded hard against the ground and felt a sudden soreness near his elbows where he had braced himself. Eugene got back to his feet and rubbed his side from the fall. He studied the root more carefully and noticed that it seemed to run above the ground for an impossibly long distance, weaving just above the earth in the direction that they were heading. Eugene couldn't understand how he missed it. More disturbing, he wasn't sure if it was some trick of the lowering sun, but the root looked patched with reddish color in the manner of thin veins.

11

"That's it!" Moss rasped excitedly, sporting a rare and ungainly smile. Eugene decided that he immediately preferred Moss's more somber and customary expression. Moss spoke again, full of confidence. "We only need to follow this for a little ways, and it'll lead us right to it."

Despite the comely grin of his guide, Eugene could feel the welling of disappointment. He could imagine Moss's Haunchyville as they followed after the unusual vein into a patch of woods. *Probably a curious circle of strange stumps and trees*, Eugene thought. *Maybe some look like little hollow dwellings, and perhaps, if Moss had any skill with woodworking, some are staged to look like miniature hovels. But if those were the only qualifications for Haunchyville, how many hundreds of "Haunchyvilles" must there be in this state alone, manufactured or otherwise?*

"Now you must keep your wits about you, Mr. Shepard. The folk who live in Haunchyville are a curious sort, but only so far as they don't feel threatened. In that state, they can be quite vicious, protective."

The way he's speaking, he believes that he has seen these creatures with his own eyes. As difficult as it was for Eugene, he now had two unlikely possibilities regarding Moss's words: that he was insane and hallucinating, or that he was telling the truth.

"Tom, what do you mean by folk? You don't mean Indians?" Eugene thought he knew the lay of the land better, but could there really be an Indian tribe, left unharassed and continuing with such practices?

"No! The little folk who live here. They're like us, and yet very different. They have mean-spirited faces and a peculiar gait like they're still just learning how to walk on two legs. They put their gnarled hands out in front them like this," he gestured, moving his arms forward with his fists down and his elbows bent at ninety degrees. "I've been told some apes walk the same way, but these fellers are hairless. They hardly make a sound either, the little buggers!"

"So you've seen one up close?" Eugene replied, with a slightly dubious tone.

"Yeah, a pair of them. They were eating something, maybe some berries or rubbish off of the ground. They spotted me, I nodded at them, and they came a little bit closer. I didn't exactly feel comfortable around them, but I stooped down on my haunches . . . like you would if you needed to talk to a frightened child, I suppose." Moss squinted, as if the thought was difficult. "Just as soon as I had done that, one of 'em drew a bit closer, and I let one play with my hat! He took off with it, and while I said before they look like mean fellers, that one had a little grin on his face as he scurried off!"

"Tom, if even half of what you're saying is true, this could be quite the unique exhibition," Eugene replied, trying to rekindle his spirit of enterprise and mask his unease. His quavering voice betrayed that it was an unsuccessful attempt, and with each step following along the strange root, he became increasingly aware of the quiet and growing darkness. His footfalls sounded like egregious protests against the natural world, although Moss's were somehow more muffled. They were now well into the small forest that Eugene could turn around and not see the end of the tree-line behind him. They had taken a path almost straight through at the beginning but now had to bend and go around some dense thickets. They did this repeatedly, and at last, the terrain opened up in front of them into something of a clearing. A weaving formation of roots joined up into an enormous stump in the center of the clearing. Unnaturally surrounding the broad stump was a ring of half-formed trees and other barren trunks, all leaning in some degree towards the center of the circle. The trees appeared lifeless, having lost all of their leaves well before their season, but their bark remained robust. Petrified, perhaps. Sure enough, nearly all of the various tree "structures" in the circle had little doorways of varying shapes, fashioned in an unknown way. The insides of the hollowed hovels were so dark that Eugene could discern almost nothing of what was inside. The one thing he could make out was that the interiors immediately started sloping down, perhaps suggesting more expansive dwellings underground. In that moment, Eugene imagined that perhaps underneath his feet all of these stumps were connected in an underground network of tunnels, and his mind returned to the role of the strange root that he and Moss had followed.

"As promised, Mr. Shepard, Haunchyville." This last word was barely more than a whisper from Moss as he carefully looked around.

While Eugene had still not seen anything expressly unique, he had decided he was genuinely impressed with the initial look of the place, although the location meant for a smaller number of guests to be accommodated. Perhaps he could arrange a partnership with a coach service for tour groups, but it was difficult for Eugene to think *business* with how uncomfortable he felt now that he had at last been brought to the place. He had felt a growing sense of unease and malice since he had tripped over that grotesque root. Eugene tried to remember the name of a story from his childhood about a forest that had a mind of its own and was distrustful of visitors. Bitterly, Eugene remembered his promise to pay Moss, and he had discovered nothing to reverse his recent misfortunes. He breathed deeply and steeled himself, knowing that he needed to go further and get as much as he could from this tiring day. His rising emotions caused him to at last blurt out, "Where are they, Tom? The . . . folks?"

Tom answered swiftly as if anticipating the exact question. "They could be hunting or sleeping. I don't rightly know if they prefer the night or the day." Moss sat with his back against a tree and grabbed some jerky out of his satchel to snack on. It dawned on Eugene that he had never actively watched Moss eat, and there was a bizarre savagery with which he noshed his food. "I would say that if they don't want you to see them, you won't get so much as a peep," Moss added.

Eugene looked up and through the canopy of branches and colored leaves above him and saw that, although the sun was only now setting, he could begin to dimly see the stars in the sky above, which had become a magnificent gradient of purple and deep red. At that moment, he regretted he did not have a better view of the western horizon and wondered what caused the odd coloration. "Moss, do you see the sky? How beautiful it is?" He faintly heard an acknowledged grunt from the man through tough chewing. Eugene was fully convinced in the special properties of this location and decided to venture toward one of these doorways with a renewed sense of inquisitiveness replacing his worry.

Eugene could hear Moss laughing as he approached one of the doors, and Moss must have said something, but Eugene couldn't make out what he had said. At one of the larger dwarf trees, Eugene hunched down onto his haunches and thought that the air coming out of the carved recess felt cold. It was quite dark, but in a few moments Eugene was able to light a small lantern that he had brought with him. The hollow of this tree was indeed marvelously deep, and a tunnel of sort descended on for some distance below. There was a pile of some rubbish further in, and something was glittering, reflecting from the light of Eugene's lantern.

"Mr. Shepard! Mr. Shepard!" Eugene had never heard Moss cry out so loudly.

Starled and alarmed, Eugene crawled back and turned himself around to come out of the entryway. He saw Moss, who was engaged in an ungainly run, truly more of a limping jog. "Moss! Where the hell are you going?"

"They've come back!" Moss whimpered without turning back to him. "I've never seen so many all at once! It can't be safe! It can't be safe!"

Eugene took a quick look around and at first saw nothing, caught between alarm and relief. *Is Moss completely daft?* Eugene's eyes frantically searched, and he was often startled by vague shapes of figures among the stunted trees, only to discover they were stumps and nothing more. But then, he discerned an unmistakable huddled mass of small, bald-looking creatures congregated around the large stump in the middle of the circle of trees, like little mushrooms that had sprouted out of the ground. They stood still, in a strange, haphazard formation, as if posing for a macabre photograph. Their lower jaws protruded out revealing large teeth, oversized for the shape of their mouth. Their flesh was pale, and they had a slight hunch, and they did not have any clothing on. All of their faces looked male, not fully human, but full of loathing. Eugene could not stand their grotesque appearance, but worse was an aura of malice, a certain seething hatred that he felt, though they had not budged since he had first spotted them. His mind raced. *Should I run? Surely I could outrun them . . .*

He had scarce more time for thought. The little pigmy-like men began creeping forward, making no utterance but maintaining the expression that Eugene had already grown to despise. They seemed to make not a sound as they stepped on leaf and twig, and the unnatural silence of their approach made the whole encounter feel like he was paralyzed in a dream state. Their eyes all locked on Eugene as he held up his lamp and stood his ground, drawing a Colt Single Action Army Revolver from a holster inside of his jacket. Eugene had had his run-ins with unsavory crowds in his line of work and was no fool to completely trust someone like Moss, and Eugene even considered that he might need protection from his unstable guide before their business was concluded.

"Moss! Get back here, you coward!" Eugene cried out, his voice weak, unable to think of anything else to say.

There was no reply from Moss, who had made a break for it. Eugene was spurred on not only to survive, but also to get back at Moss, and he fired one shot straight into the air to try and disperse the encroaching enemies. Eugene half expected the crushing and dreadful silence to stifle the gunshot, but it rang out clearly, and they froze in their tracks. Eugene began backpedaling, keeping his eyes on the creatures, leveling his gun at them. It seemed to have grown darker in the eternity since these hellish creatures had emerged, and Eugene had increasing trouble discerning the creatures against the stumps and growth that they were creeping around as they resumed following him.

Eugene squeezed the trigger of his pistol two more times, aiming squarely for the one that was closest to him. It dropped to the ground, and Eugene turned and ran. He could hear the abandonment of the stealthy pursuit behind him, replaced by a multitude of pattering footfalls that sounded much like a strong wind upturning detritus and fallen leaves. Eugene hoped that, through sheer size, he could outrun them. Yet the sudden and damnable darkness, perhaps thanks to a conspiracy of the canopy of half-leaved branches above, concealed all of the treacherous roots and uneven terrain that

Eugene and Moss had taken care to avoid on the way in. For the second time, Eugene tripped on some unseen snare and hit the ground hard, his lamp shattering at the base of a nearby tree. He wrenched up, and it looked like the whole forest was alive with movement. Nothing was discernible, and all shapes represented unknown horrors that shambled about. The increased darkness made Eugene aware of a dim, sallow light, like the glow of a strange lichen, emanating out of the tree houses and stumps that he could still see somewhat distantly. He turned his back to the infernal site and ran.

Eugene desperately bungled through the wood and frequently whipped around and looked for more creatures or to fire one of his remaining pistol rounds. He was sweating and delirious, questioning how he had brought himself into this nightmare. Eugene had fired his last shot, and to his horror, seemed to be approaching the same place, spotting the dim light in the circle of hunched trees. Eugene was not sure whether survival instinct or madness gripped him, but he made a break for one of the hovels. *They can't surround me in here. I can have my back to a wall. They'll learn to leave me alone. Then I'll find him. I'll find Moss.*

Eugene scuttled into the shaped tunnel, discovering that the source of the pale light seemed to come from the living walls of the stumped tree itself. There was a faint but foul smell in there, and somehow it felt colder than the outside. He could hear movement behind him in the clearing, but he saw that the tunnel led somewhere deeper below. Eugene cursed, then prayed, then crawled.

1

The persistent mists blanketed the streets with mystery. On the night of October 16, a piercing wind swept over Roger Merrick, biting through his coat. Streetlamps rattled and creaked, adding to the orchestral whispers of flying leaves. Upon his arrival, Roger found Waukesha, Wisconsin to be a quaint town compared to the Windy City, but it had a certain charm, even in the final waning of its tourist season for the year. The city was mute and dim compared to Chicago, but it had many charming buildings and a certain delectable air. Roger finished his stroll from the train stop to the National Hotel.

As Roger stepped inside, he found the lobby luxuriously furnished, featuring electric lighting—no guarantee for lodging in a town of this size. After confirming his reservation and politely enduring the staff worker's inquiries and comments about a "bigtime Chicago reporter," Roger went to his room on the second floor. The room had a northwestern-facing window with a view of the street and the Fox River. Roger smiled at the marked increase in comfort over his transportation arrangements. He had been denied one of the three automobiles owned by the *Tribune*;

while the car was practical for a trip to Milwaukee, the roads to Waukesha were not yet serviceable. Roger would therefore have to wait for his first spin in the new *Mitchel* automobile manufactured out of Racine. The principal coverage team was still on their way back from New York City after covering the World Series, and the trip represented a potential "big break" for the aspiring journalist. The train service to Milwaukee proved excellent, although the line to Waukesha had been delayed and cramped. As Roger sat on the bed and unlaced his shoes, he recalled his discussion with his supervising editor about the assignment the previous day.

"It's a fairly standard assignment," Lou Baker began through the difficulty of cradling a fat cigar in his mouth. Rain pattered hard against the fourth-story window of the *Tribune* building. "Therein lies the stamp of a true journalist, though, articulating the compelling in the ordinary! I had some statistics for you . . . somewhere, that annual traffic is way down of late to Spring City," he said, with a hint of condescension. "I believe the big attraction, the Fountain Spring House, was started by an investor out of Chicago, so there's always been a bit of a connection. Your story should give folks something interesting to think about while they plan their leisure for next summer. They are planning further and further advance, I tell you!"

"Lou, you went there a few years ago didn't you?" Roger replied, looking over a brochure of the Fountain Spring House, and taking interest in the relaxed description of men and women "sharing trivialities, spring water, and spirits together in the summertime heat!"

"Oh yeah, felt great on my knees! A miracle treatment though? I don't think I'd call it that, but you do get caught up with the culture of it all. Plus, you might run into a few celebrity patients . . . uh . . . patrons, over there. At least, you used to anyway. Try to get some interviews!"

"Is there a spin that you're looking for on this one?"

"No, no spins! You've done some good work so far Roger—real journalism I'd daresay!" Lou set his cigar down on a silver tray and scratched the back of his head. He checked his fingertips and flicked off some flakes, taking no heed of Roger, and then leaned back, his chair creaking beneath him as he tucked his thumbs under his suspender straps. "You're going to want to be thorough, though, so please resist any low-hanging fruit of half-boiled information or hearsay. The whole livelihood of this town is at stake; it could practically be off the map in a decade if their beloved springs tourism dries up." Lou quickly smiled at his turn-of-phrase. "You can take a week or so if you want to. We've hit a bit of a slow patch. Mark down some research for several side stories, too. Your hotel has a telephone in case any breaking stories or important updates arise. We've included up to three calls in your allotment; the rest will be on your dime!"

Roger neatly gathered the folder of materials, contact information, and trip expenditure allowance from the *Tribune* as he finished his glass of bourbon that Lou had poured for him. Roger regarded Lou's open-handedness with spirits as one of his redeeming traits. Sometimes he would refill the glass if he was in a particularly good mood. Roger was about to leave until he noticed an article title in the folder from the *Waukesha Freeman*, dated September 22 of that year.

"Someone reported traumatic skin irritation from the spring water," Roger began, "or inflammation from drinking it, the wording's unclear . . . and later died of complications at a hospital in Milwaukee," he added, alarmed. "That's some pretty bad press already, if it's true."

"But it can't account entirely for their slump," Lou responded, resting his chin on his free hand as he glanced down at another report. "I remember when they rebuilt from that arsonist's work in the late '70s, but they've been in a bad way for a couple of years now, before that recent story broke out. Far from the 'Saratoga of the West,' as they like to advertise. You do raise a good point though. A follow-up on that incident could help get you started. In any case, you're going to be holding some reputations in your hands, Roger. I don't know how much of their business comes from Chicago, but that should open some doors for you." He paused as he exhaled a particularly large plume of smoke. A dog barked somewhere outside on the street, and Lou refocused himself. "Just bring back something worth reading."

Roger's thoughts returned to the present as he readied himself for bed in his hotel room. He brought out his folder once again, recently bolstered by the last two weeks of *Freeman* editions. The local news seemed preoccupied with the fate of the springs, with tidbits about the environmental impact of utilizing spring water for resorts and logistical concerns of bottling and exporting the water. Roger discovered yet more connections with sewage issues in the Fox River, and a few old-standing religious and territorial claims by Indian groups to tracts of land and waterways in the area which, according to some, required further resolution. As Roger prepared to shut the folder, his eye caught a glimmer of another article from a month ago titled, *"Fearsome Critter Hodag: fact or fiction? An Interview with Eugene Shepard,"* by Ryan Stanley. *What the hell is a Hodag?* Roger thought as he perused the story, recalling the name as he looked at a photograph from 1893 of the purported capture.

Shepard admitted in the interview with Stanley that the now proven hoax was in "jovial humor" and that the invention allowed another folly for Oneida County fairgoers to enjoy.

"Wisconsin is a beautiful state, with its own developing legends," Shepard added, "and the fearsome critter of the Hodag reminds us of our old frontier heritage, protecting our farmsteads, bringing domestication to the North Woods and our beautiful state. It's even in some Paul Bunyan stories. I heard a lumberjack in a bar in North Dakota mention one last year!" Shepard declined to comment on how he precisely staged the photograph and design of the creature, owing to trade secrets of an entertainer. This, however, had not discouraged Shepard from "thoroughly investigating" any and all claims of mythical or supernatural accounts within his state as his personal mission. Shepard intended to investigate the legend of "Haunchyville" in the Waukesha area over the upcoming weeks, promising to bring added publicity to the town. Roger stiffened at the unoriginal name of "Haunchyville," yet finished his reading of the article, feeling bemused. He laid down to sleep that night. For a while, he tried to imagine what a real Hodag could look like, and many forms danced and shifted in his head. When this exercise had run its course, Roger passed into a dreamless sleep.

When Roger awoke the next morning, he compiled some notes and questions for his only appointed interview with the daytime manager of the Fountain Spring House. He enjoyed breakfast in leisure at the hotel's restaurant while waiting for his scheduled interview at 9:30 in the morning. Just after nine, he strolled out the door to a fine Saturday morning, a contrast to the ominous aura of the streets the night before. It took a fifteen-minute walk, southeast down Broadway Street from the hotel, to arrive at the large plot of the Fountain Spring House, although its careful landscaping showed some signs of overgrowth. There were carefully mown lawns for picnics, numerous outer springs that were now derelict in the increasingly chillier days, and tennis courts in the distance. The race track for the hounds was inactive, but the grand main building looked like something of a parliament or government structure, with rows of symmetrical windows looking out of the stone, two-story edifice. An architectural flourish of the design was a stately spiral tower at one corner of the structure. The Spring House had many guest rooms, although it would not house visitors until the resuming of the prime season in the spring.

Currently, only a small portion of the building remained in operation for the waning of the autumnal season.

As Roger entered, he could feel a refreshing moisture in the air and a comfortable warmth; this branch of the building was near a pair of springs pools, accessible just off of the main corridor. He removed his hat and was greeted warmly by the receptionist at the desk—Ms. Cynthia Lowell, a young woman in her early twenties wearing square-rimmed glasses and her auburn hair bundled in an immaculate bun. She noted that while it was a particularly busy morning (although Roger noted the premises seemed well below capacity), the general manager was still available for the interview. Roger helped himself to a seat while he waited for the manager.

"Rheumatism? A little congestion in the lungs?" a man's voice asked Roger from a nearby seat. The man was athletic, wearing a form-fitting buttoned shirt with one loosened just below the collar and casual pants. "Name's Peaches, Peaches Graham. Maybe you've heard of me? Play a little ball for the Cubbies at pitcher, but I've also played catcher for Cleveland! I like to start my off-seasons with a trip up here. They have a bar too, of course! More than one in fact," he said grinning, holding a juiced cocktail aloft.

"Thank you, Joseph!" Peaches remarked to a Black man wearing a formal suit and bow tie, who walked by with an empty serving tray back over to the bar. As the man began mixing another drink, he gave a friendly nod back to the baseball player.

"I recommend mixing the spring water with a little spirit

if you really want a refresher!" Peaches remarked. " Scotch is the best match, if you can afford it."

"Mr. Peaches." Roger spoke the unusual name trippingly. "You happen to be speaking to a fellow Chicagoan!" Roger produced his notebook, resting his right ankle on his left knee, bringing his leg up as was his custom while writing. "Roger Merrick, for the *Tribune*, at your service. How many years have you made the trip to Waukesha, if you don't mind?"

"Well look at you! Looks like not everyone gets to come here for leisure!" Peaches laughed. "This will be my . . . third year. Ms. Lucy runs a very professional outfit here. Plus, there's all sorts of great folks you can mingle with . . . and most folks who know a lick about baseball up here are Cubs fans!"

"Great! Have you noticed a bit of . . . a "drop off" in the number of patrons from when you first started coming here, Mr. Graham?"

"You know, as a matter of fact, I have. And just call me Peaches," he said, stretching his legs out and folding his hands behind his head. Roger got the impression this may have been a rare interview opportunity for Peaches, who didn't seem to mind that it wasn't about his ball-playing expertise. "Last year, one gentleman said he was looking to vacation elsewhere, taking advantage of his new automobile. I think he said he was heading further west, or somewhere that was warmer, year-round."

"Mr. Merrick?" a clear voice asked. Roger turned and saw that the Spring House manager had entered the front room. Lucy Morris was a woman who fit the description that Roger once heard as a "tall drink of water," with black curly hair worn down, and piercing green eyes. She looked perhaps only a few years older than her receptionist. She was wearing a form-fitting checkered suit that came down to her ankles, rendering a professional look that left Roger positively charmed, forgetting everything for a moment as he just smiled.

"Please excuse me, Mr. Graham," Roger said, leafing past a few blank pages of his notebook in anticipation of his appointment. "Let's catch up again soon. We had only sat down, and I'd very much like to feature you in the *Tribune*."

"I'll be here all week, pal!" Peaches replied, heading towards one of the baths.

"Allow me to give you a tour, Mr. Merrick. We can walk and talk, perhaps?" she said, still smiling.

"Of course, Ms. Morris, let's see . . ." Roger cleared his throat, and his tone of voice shifted. "Chicagoans have an increasing range of vacation vistas at their disposal. What makes Waukesha, often called "Spring City," a destination of interest for discerning citizens who value their leisure time?"

Lucy Morris did not immediately answer but began escorting Roger down the main hallway of the House. "You'll have to discover the answer to that question firsthand of course," she replied. "I hope you brought a bathing suit. Please take advantage of one of our fine changing rooms before we head to the attached bathhouse," she finished, with a sweeping gesture, almost a bow, as her long fingers pointed through an open doorway. Roger had the presence of mind to bring a suit with, although he had no appropriate footwear. He stepped into one of the changing rooms that had a long, finely-carved wooden bench with lockers while Ms. Morris waited out in the hallway. As he emerged, he felt a bit silly standing in his swimwear with no stockings, but he was also holding his pen and notepad.

"Bare feet are just fine, Mr. Merrick!" Ms. Morris said with a light laugh. "Right this way. Did you know that our Fountain Spring House has been attracting visitors since the early '70s? If anything is ailing you, you are sure to relieve any aching bones or maladies through drink or bathing. If not, you should feel revitalized after even a short time here. Furthermore, for a news man such as yourself, you should take a look at this, one of our little badges of honor." In a glass frame mounted on the wall was an 1872 clipping from the *Milwaukee Sentinel* newspaper. It read, "The use of Bethesda water is no longer an experiment. No one can converse with a tithe of the hundreds now in Waukesha without being convinced of the spring water's miraculous powers," this last phrase being narrated melodiously by Lucy.

"Charming!" Roger responded, forming a cautious smile. "Do you claim exclusivity, or is there competition in the healing waters market?"

"Certainly this isn't the only springs house, even in the area," she answered, returning the grin. "Although we offer a distinguished service and drinking-water quality compared to the other dozen or so you'd find in the city, even the nation. Our science is based solely on customer satisfaction and recovery. If one of our many contented patrons describes this process as miraculous, they are more than welcome to that view. It has been said that the Lord may work in mysterious ways. Now, why don't you see for yourself, Mr. Merrick?"

Roger set aside his pen and pad and lowered himself gingerly into the water, his toes curling from the heat. He sat on an inlaid bench and the water came up to his neck. Roger began sweating, but it was a comfortable sweat, and his muscles began loosening up; his very spirit felt in equilibrium. He closed his eyes and felt a glass of spring water carefully placed into his hand, and it felt soothing on his throat as he drank. He leaned his head back on the cold stone floor above the pool, and for a moment, cleared his mind and forgot about all of his obligations, feeling lighter from his head down to his toes and totally insulated from the outside cold or worrying thoughts.

"You look very comfortable, Mr. Merrick!" Lucy offered, pleasantly.

"Oh, um, yes, Ms. Morris! I'm sorry, I had forgotten myself. It is a lovely experience. In fact, my heel doesn't feel nearly as tight. Although, I expect that I would feel much the same relief in any body of water that is sufficiently warm. I understand that the springs are not naturally hot, so you must have a boiler or heating system nearby for your bathhouses?"

"If you're forgetting yourself, you're catching on to the point!" She said, smiling. "But as to your second point, that is where I think you are wrong, Mr. Merrick." Lucy's tone was still pleasant, but firm. She strutted to the far side of the pool looking directly across at Roger. "I don't know how thorough you intend to be with your journalism, but if you find a better or more relaxing spring, you must bring it to my attention. But I won't likely believe it!"

Roger frowned since his more difficult follow-ups had to be aired. "Ms. Morris, I do know that your returning patrons are in decline—it's no secret. I'm trying to report as to why that is. As I said, this is all perfectly lovely, but people must be finding satisfaction at other destinations as well. As of this moment, I can't see what should make the Waukesha Springs so special apart from convenience . . . now please don't give me that look! Your accommodations here will still earn high marks from the *Tribune*! But would you care to comment, Ms. Morris? I'd like to hear your perspective on why you think the city's resorts have fallen on hard times. Of course, I must mention that one incident reported not long ago of agitation from the waters of the spring connected to the . . . death of a patron."

"That was merely unsubstantiated drivel from the *Freeman*!" she replied with animus. "That was never proven to be the cause of that poor fellow's demise. He clearly had some pre-existing conditions and should never have gotten into a hot pool to begin with—probably something wrong with his heart or the exertion of bending over too quickly! We had a hydrologist test the waters, and he found nothing wrong with them. I can show you his report!" Lucy sighed, and spoke more calmly. "As far as the other reasons, I don't rightly know, Mr. Merrick. There are some folks in town who will tell you that they know for certain, although none of them will agree on any one thing. Why do people vacation to one spot over the other? I suppose we all enjoy some variety . . . and medical practitioners are always innovating and prescribing new treatments that aim to replace more natural methods." Lucy stroked her hands back through her hair, pushing it away from her eyes along with the moisture from her brow, and Roger hesitated to interject. "Not all things are meant to last. But you can be sure, Mr. Merrick, that while I have clients, I will run the best springs resort this side of the Mississippi River, and you can put that in your article!" She spoke strongly and began walking back towards the doorway. "Take as long as you like, Mr. Merrick. You have been given the courtesy of a day pass, but I must be attending to other matters for now."

Roger got partly out of the springs so that only his legs beneath the knees remained submerged. He had some notes to jot down regarding his interview, and while his short-term memory was excellent, he had developed the healthy habit of never letting much time pass before writing; he preferred his thoughts fresh. Roger had just finished his glass of spring water when he concluded that his notes were woefully short of what he had hoped. The door to the bath opened, and Peaches joined him by the side of the pool.

"Not a bad place, 'ey Pal? Little bit sparse now. I hear that during the summer there are gals everywhere, unattended! They call it the 'trysting spot!'" he added, his expression distant and dreaming. "One major drawback of the long baseball season I suppose. I can never make it then! They ought to form a club up here, and then I'd be in business!"

"Ah . . . Mr. uh, Peaches. I agree, it is quite a refreshing spot. So, Peaches, how much do the springs help you in preparing for the next season?"

"Help me? Hmm, not sure how much it helps me. It sure feels nice on the arm, though, after throwing all of those games. It hasn't increased my speed, if that's what you mean. Maybe I'm not cut out to pitch, but I think I could keep playing ball. Maybe go back to catcher. But say, how much of the town have you seen, Roger?"

"Very little. I just arrived last evening. Apart from my hotel and the Spring House here, the city is all but unknown to me."

"You've got to let me show you around; there are a few local fellows you really should meet. You'll get a better picture of the town after we go out."

Peaches was not Roger's usual sort of company, although he seemed like a decent enough fellow, and Roger was curious to explore further. He would need to supplement his thin material with anything he could muster. "I think I've had about enough soaking for now," Roger replied as he finished some moderate embellishments to Peaches's account of his off-season routine in his notes. "And I think that a night on the town sounds splendid."

Roger confirmed his hotel with Peaches, where the two agreed to meet for cocktails that evening. From there, Peaches assured Roger that there were several establishments that he needed to see before he could "call it a trip" to Waukesha. Roger would only bring his smallest notepad and avoid his most formal clothes. As he went down into the lobby, he was informed by the maître d of a phone call that was currently on hold for him. Roger expected that it was his boss, Lou, but instead, it was a professor of history and geography from Carroll College, just down the street. The man, Reginald Linden, had heard that a Chicago journalist was in town and offered some information that Roger might find interesting regarding local history and the springs. By the time Roger had finalized the appointment with Linden for the next morning, he saw that his new friend Peaches was waving one hand at him from a bar counter, the other hand already cupping a drink. He smiled as Roger sat down next to him.

"So, whadaya drinking, Roger?"

"Let's go with an Old Fashioned," Roger replied, after hearing the name of the beverage mentioned by someone earlier.

"I thought you'd be an Old Fashioned sort," Peaches chuckled. "But remember, they make it with brandy here! The beer isn't bad here either. Most folks swear by Miller beer, and you can even find it in some Chicago establishments now. The Pabst variety is my preference."

"I've had Miller. It is a fine draft," Roger said as he grabbed his Old Fashioned off of the counter. "If I were in the area longer, there are a number of different places I'd like to see."

"I've only passed through Milwaukee myself," Peaches replied. "So you're just doing a piece on the Spring House? Nothing else?"

"That's the gist of it. I'm trying to uncover what the situation is regarding its future. It hasn't been doing so well."

"No, it has not," an unknown voice added, as a black-haired gentleman with a long, full beard sat beside Roger. Evidently, he had caught their conversation. "A rather dated component of our fair city, if you ask me. A bit too sprawling. The Fox and local water resources should be channeled for more productive means. Bradley Evers, of Evers Automation, at your service!" the man finished, extending an uncomfortably firm handshake to Roger.

"A captain of industry then?" Roger asked with a bit of a smirk, forgetting to introduce himself.

"You're too kind!" Evers raised one foot up onto the lower bar of his barstool, folding his hands as if trying against his very nature to look relaxed or friendly. To Roger, it seemed the man was doing his best to measure up this visiting journalist. "Your reputation in town already precedes you, Mr. Merrick."

That surprised Roger, and not in a pleasant way. He was increasingly vexed by the news of his presence spreading like wildfire. Additionally, there was something unsettling about Evers, a type of deep-seated ruthlessness in his stare.

"I'll cut right to the point," Evers began. "You know tourism here is in trouble. Take the Fountain Spring House. It merely needs a little more time and it will collapse on its own, to be sold off, closed, or demolished. Writing a sympathetic puff-piece is only going to make its exit more prolonged, even painful. Just take a walk down Broadway, and you'll see plenty of attractive historic buildings. I would merely advise you to highlight that the natural features surrounding our town ought to be put to better use. Namely, expansion of manufacturing, creating growth and prosperity." He paused to take a healthy swig of a clear drink, then continued. "It's for the best that the waterways be used to vent byproducts and contaminants. We have more than enough vacation real estate potential along the shore of Lake Michigan. Imagine one metropolis someday connecting Chicago, Milwaukee, Waukesha, even Madison, all through venture capitalism! I'm not asking for a specific endorsement of Evers Automation, but certain mentions that arise . . . organically . . . have rewarding considerations!" He finished with an unnaturally wide smile, sporting his thoroughly yellow teeth.

Roger faced ahead, looking at the bar, and had some more of his Old Fashioned. After letting out a sigh, he said, "Well, you should know that my journalism isn't for sale, Mr. Evers. I should also mention that approaching me in this manner only convinces me that something may indeed be amiss regarding your business practices." Roger regretted the statement immediately, unsure of where his bravado was coming from. He interrupted himself by taking another quick sip to prepare his next sentence. "But you can rest assured, I won't report anything, um, misleading. I'm gathering a range of perspectives for the pleasure of *Tribune* subscribers."

Evers stood up and leaned forward, one leg bending as he planted one foot on Roger's barstool, with one hand gripping the bar counter and the other closing into a fist. It was apparent that he was indeed a large man, more muscular than most entrepreneurs, Roger imagined. Evers's face couldn't have been more than a foot away from Roger as he continued his toothy grin. "Very admirable, but you Chicagoans should keep to your own affairs." He snarled the words through his teeth. "You'll regret it if you cause me any trouble with your damned stories." Evers rose from his seat, apparently satisfied with his message. "Enjoy your stay in Waukesha." As he walked away, two other men who had been sitting at another table abruptly stood up and followed him.

"Well, that man is about as charming as our tobacco bucket after extra innings!" Peaches offered, who also seemed to have finished his drink.

"I didn't expect this story to generate this kind of controversy among the locals," Roger began, "although I see that there are some agendas in play here, and probably other ones I'm not aware of yet."

"Well, now it feels stuffy in here. Shall we move on, Roger?"

Roger and Peaches left the hotel bar. Peaches led them through the streets, which were mostly empty, although the night was warmer than yesterday and less damp. Once again, Roger was unaccustomed to the relative quiet compared to Chicago. Peaches had them popping into one place after the other, usually with a comment of "bartender's a good man" or "spirited folks here." One was themed after a German *bierhaus*, but according to Peaches they had more grand ones in Milwaukee which are often packed to the brim. At each stop, Roger had one drink, and Peaches usually had two or three. After another couple of hours and pubs, they arrived at a place called McGinty's, as most of the more reputable lounges had closed by now. Roger could feel the liquor going to his head, and he wasn't accustomed to Peaches's seasoned pace; although, so far Peaches had proven to be a good companion. A little after midnight they walked into the Irish pub, and it seemed to be a peak time for the establishment. Roger and Peaches immediately noticed that there were even a few women inside. Roger felt that he was nearing his limit and was unsure of how far they were from his hotel. Peaches brought them over to the bar counter, which had just enough room for the two of them to squeeze in.

"Good God, that Lucy Morris!" Peaches recollected dreamily, with a noticeable slur. "She doesn't seem to be a married woman. How has a gal like her gone without finding a man for so long? And running a business operation, no less?"

"Maybe she does not want a husband," Roger said flatly, not knowing what else to say. "Do you have designs on her, Peaches?" Roger redirected with an awkward smile.

"Oh, I couldn't do that to you, friend!" Peaches grinned after Roger started blushing. The baseball player laughed as he failed to be persuaded by Roger that the latter's complexion change was from the drinks. "I can see you're rather taken with her, although I don't exactly know how many pretty women a man of your line of work runs into." A flustered Roger tried to respond, but Peaches kept going, waving his hand. "I don't imagine it working out with us anyway. I travel farther than a reporter like you. I more had my eye on that receptionist, but she's engaged to be married."

"What about at your baseball games? Surely there are some women drawn to athletes such as yourself?" Roger asked.

Peaches finished his drink with some gasping, then laughed hard. "Baseball games, hah! No better way to clear out a mile radius of any good-looking women! Maybe someday we'll have a more . . . diverse crowd of admirers. But hell, making a living wage playing a game? A man could do worse." Peaches's attention was already drifting to one of the ladies across the tavern, who was conversing with a few gentlemen whose backs were turned away from Roger.

"Hello strangers," said a middle-aged man who sensed an opening in Peaches's dialogue at the neighboring barstool. He had long black hair that came down to his broad shoulders and had a tan complexion. "The name's Sam. Please forgive my interruption. You look familiar to me," he said, gesturing to Peaches, who wasn't listening at the moment. "But I'm quite sure I've never seen your face before," he said as he turned to Roger.

"Roger Merrick, reporter for the *Chicago Tribute*. No . . . *Tribune*." Roger corrected, dizzily. "My friend is Peaches Graham, pitcher for the Chicago Cubs." Peaches smiled and offered a token greeting, then quickly turned his head to try and draw the attention of the bartender.

"You both have that Chicago accent," said Sam with a bit of a smile. "I have a farm and a bit of land . . . no, it's not a reservation," he clarified, reading the confusion in Roger's expression. "The Ho-Chunk Nation of Wisconsin has been slowly returning after many were pushed west in the early 1800s. I went to school in Black River Falls, and my family was given the plot I now reside on through the Homestead Act in 1870. Then there was the Dawes Act, and we received citizenship almost a decade later. As an elder, you could say I try to keep the Ho-Chunk community in the area active. Do you encounter many Indians down in Chicago, Mr. Merrick?

"Can't say that I do, Sam," Roger replied, haltingly. He was surprised at not only finding women, but Indians in the bar, but that had not been the cause of his jarred speech. Roger's mind was swimming, and he had a headache. This was precisely the kind of perspective he wished to add, but the journalist was in no proper condition to conduct an interview. Out of fear that he might drop it somewhere, he kept his notepad stowed away.

"You can speak frankly, Roger. It seems like something is on your mind," Sam replied, graciously.

Roger relaxed a bit. He realized how tiring it had been to keep up his professional appearance. "Sam, I like Waukesha well enough, but everyone seems convinced I'm about to ruin them. I don't want to be the public enemy around town. What's their deal?"

"Ah," Sam said. "You're from out of town and a reporter,

so everyone's trying to grab your ear. I expect that should calm down in a bit. Depending on how long you're in town, there is something tomorrow evening you may be interested in. Might allow you to relax or even give you another story."

Peaches handed Roger a drink, saying that this round was on him. Roger had completely lost count at that point. He took one look at the drink and nearly vomited when thinking about throwing it back, and he decided to leave it on the counter for the moment. "What is this . . . something, Sam?"

"Well, as I said, I have about fourteen hectares on the outskirts of town. We're going to have a powwow out there tomorrow night, welcome to anyone who wants to come, probably the last one for the year, with the weather. A lot of the Ho-Chunk are Christian now, so it's not strictly religious. We encourage whoever wants to attend to show solidarity in our community while we celebrate the traditions of our ancestors, our culture. We have a number of people who occasionally attend from outside the tribe." Sam's face brightened as he apparently remembered something. "Usually have a bit of a bonfire to wrap things up afterward, a popular activity at this time of year! You may run into a few more interested parties maybe?"

"Appreciate the invitation," Roger airily replied as he looked over at a vaguely familiar man across the bar who he couldn't quite place. "I think I shall take you up on that. Say, Sam, do you know that fellow over there?" Roger gestured over to a man who looked unpleasant and familiar.

Sam took a glance, and his face soured slightly. "Yeah, his name is Jim something . . . Smitheran, maybe. He's an associate of that big-slick, Brad Evers. This normally ain't his type of place. You already on the wrong side of big business?" he said, his smile returning.

"I hope not, although I should probably be getting back soon. I'm afraid I need to either cut off Peaches here or head back to my hotel on my own."

"You're sure you can tell a man like Peaches when he's had enough?" Sam replied gently.

"Peaches," Roger leaned in toward his companion, and nearly dropped his watch as he retrieved it from his pocket. "What do you say we call it a night? It's almost one in the morning, and if I remember correctly, we have a ways to go to get back to the hotel."

"Sure thing, Roger!" Peaches said while holding a new drink. "Lemme polish this one off, and we can call it a night." He finished about half of his drink in a large gulp, then noticed Roger's nearly full drink sitting in front of him. "Don't forget about yours there, friend!" he added, downing the rest of his. "Just excuse me to the latrine for a moment." Peaches slowly rose and made his way to the bathroom. Roger had his eye on Jim Smitheran who also started to get up out of his seat but decided to sit back down when he noticed that Roger had not moved, and the two made brief and unpleasant eye contact.

"I'm afraid that Smitheran fellow definitely has it out for us, in one way or another. I'm more concerned whether he has some friends with him that I haven't spotted yet," Roger said, trying to look inconspicuous as he scanned the room, realizing he could do neither all that well in his condition.

"Things normally aren't so exciting around here," Sam responded, still smiling. "Tell you what, Roger, I'll keep an eye on you guys when you leave. To be honest, there are a few folks around here, like anywhere, who don't seem to like Indians, Negros, or whoever they don't like sharing this good Earth with. But I don't think they'll be so bold to try anything if I join your group unless there's truly a posse after you. It is a bit of a walk for me back to my house, so I can't go with you all of the way."

"Thanks, Sam. Come to think of it, I could use a stop in the bathroom as well." Roger grimaced as he polished off the rest of his drink and stumbled past a few other patrons, but the bar was now thinning out considerably, and his route was no longer as crowded. As Roger entered the bathroom, which had a four-privy bench with dividers for privacy, he could hear gentle snoring. In the first privy, he could see Peaches propped up against one of the dividing walls, sleeping peacefully with his head perilously close to the seat. As Roger drew nearer, he scrunched up his face at the various odors, either from his friend or the privy below, placed one hand on his shoulder, and began lightly tapping the side of his friend's cheek with the other.

"Peaches! Peaches! Come now, my good fellow. This is no place to be sleeping!" Peaches made a retching sound as he started awake, although his eyes only opened halfway.

"Am I up? They must have moved me up the batting order! God, this dugout smells like a midden!"

"Well, uh, it is a . . . midden of sort, Peaches," Roger replied, progressively becoming more annoyed. "Damn it man, they could arrest you for public intoxication at this rate!"

"Roger? Oh blazes, sorry about that pal! I just need a moment to clear my head . . . and we'll be off."

Roger and Peaches both took some time to relieve themselves, and he heard Peaches retching. Roger was struggling to remember when his appointment was with Linden, and resigned himself to the possibility that he would be late. When they reentered the main bar area, only Sam, who had been watching the door to the bathroom, and a handful of other patrons remained. Jim Smitheran was nowhere to be seen. Peaches and Roger settled their final tab, and the negotiation with the bartender over the specifics of the bill was less than pleasant. Roger was nonetheless relieved that they were finally beginning the return journey back to the hotel.

Roger welcomed the refreshing colder air compared to the crowded bar. He felt less nauseous, but his legs were wobbly. Sam walked with them for about five minutes and then wished them well as he went on his way. While Sam was confident there would be no trouble tonight, Roger wasn't so sure, but at least it was simple enough to walk back in the direction of the city's brighter main avenues. At this point, Roger noticed that Peaches was casually tossing a baseball into the air as he walked and was astonished he had the coordination to do so. As Roger opened his mouth to remark and launch an inquiry as to where the hell his friend had produced the ball from, it changed to a gasp as a man appeared from an adjacent alley.

Roger had a moment to recognize Jim Smitheran who had turned from a shadowy corner right in front of them and blocked their way, planting his feet squarely in a wide stance. Two more fellows appeared right behind them from some other neighboring alleyway. One of them had an oversized bowler hat that hid most of his facial features, while the other was much heavier set, with a face like an ox. None of them seemed to be brandishing weapons, but that did not relieve Roger's choking tenseness over the situation. If Roger had his preference, a back-alley brawl would be near the last place he would want to be on this Earth. Roger was a bit taller than most men but also skinnier, and was not puny by any standard. He was, however, completely averse to fighting and had never had an opportunity to prove himself in a brawl. Even with Peaches there, he had a mind to prevent any bout and make whatever promises or necessary concessions to the thugs to get them to go away. As he suspected, it appeared that his companion would have none of that, and Roger would have no choice but to muster his courage.

"Oh for Pete's sake," Peaches began, "are you lads just about done following us around?" The belligerent baseball player rolled up his sleeves unevenly while asking the question. "Because if you're going to start a fight, you should get on with it already!" Peaches had displayed more energy at this moment than he had since the evening began.

Jim Smitherman hesitated, then grinned, took a boxing stance and bounced slowly towards Peaches. Roger looked at Peaches and jerked his head to make sure that his friend was also aware of the two brutes behind them. Peaches seemed to understand the gesture and wasted no time going into what must have been his pitching form. He wound up, nearly toppling over, but managed to stay on his feet as he released the ball and pelted Smitheran square in the nose with his baseball before the man could raise his hands to block. Roger himself was surprised at this surreal feat and nearly forgot about the other two brutes, who charged. His heart racing and his legs weak, Roger put up his guard as best he could; he did an odd but rather feisty sideways shuffle to avoid any blows. The technique worked, and the assailants seemed amused by the display, deciding that Peaches represented the real threat.

Peaches was handling himself splendidly. He immediately pounced on Smitheran after clocking him in the nose with the baseball, pounding his stunned for a few more times in the face with his fists for good measure. Smitheran was already down, shielding his eyes with one hand and weakly waving his other hand in defense and grunting. Peaches relented and sprung back around, but not quite in time, as the other two had rushed him. The ox-faced man was throwing heavy punches at Peaches, and whenever one connected a *pop* echoed through the alley, and it looked that Peaches might topple over from the force. Roger noticed that the other man wearing the bowler hat had just pulled out a knife; the reporter steeled himself and rejoined the fray. Following pure instinct, Roger folded his hands together and slammed his fists down as hard as he could on the man's wrist that held the blade. The man, either focused on Peaches or blinded by his oversized bowler, did not dodge Roger's attack. The blow knocked the knife free; Roger took this chance to grab the man as he was reaching down for his knife. Roger was around the same size of the man he just grappled and, was fortunate enough to only take flailing and glancing blows from the restrained man. The pain of these hits were numbed by the alcohol, and the exchange would hopefully give Peaches an even playing field against the hulk.

Peaches finally found an opening against his foe, ducking under an attack and punching the man in the gut. In a lightning motion, Peaches pivoted his foot to turn his back to the stunned brute. He quickly arched his arms behind him to grab hold of one the ox-faced man's arms, in what Roger recognized as a setup of a shoulder throw, but then Peaches grimaced. "You must weigh a goddamn ton!" Peaches cried out, suddenly stopping the motion and instead was grabbed by the behemoth, who lifted him off the ground. Roger still managed to hang on to his opponent, who was desperately trying to snatch his knife off the ground, preventing Roger from coming to his friend's aid. As Peaches was lifted into the air, he swung his shoe upward, kicking the man squarely in the groin. The ox-faced man toppled over and Peaches, landing on his feet, threw a glance back at Roger, who had just about lost all grip on his adversary. Peaches dashed for the glittering steel on the ground, grabbing it and pointing the tip right at the neck of the man who had nearly freed himself from Roger. His hat had been knocked from him, revealing a very scraggly, almost wild appearance. With the blade at his neck he froze up, and the recovering galoot who was bent over with his hands on his knees looked to be in no fighting spirit. Peaches broke the quick silence.

"Good brawl lads! Same time again tomorrow?" Peaches rasped these words, blood streaking down his face, and one of his eyes was almost swollen completely shut. "I'll hang onto this! Just might keep it!" he said, holding up the knife in the air. "Where's my ball?!" he exclaimed, and Roger was unsure if his companion actually expected an answer in return from the brutes. There was one sudden movement, a quick scooping by the man who had carried the knife, but it was merely to pick up his hat, and he began inspecting it with the utmost care. Roger scurried to his friend's side, and wordlessly, they began in the opposite direction from their assailants. Roger continually looked over his shoulder, and it appeared that the thugs were dispirited enough and did not continue their pursuit.

At this point, Roger became aware of his injuries. The top of his foot throbbed thanks to the stomping shoe of the unkempt fellow that he grappled with, and he had some bruises on his face, as well as a growing soreness spreading in his arms. Overall, he counted himself lucky, although the adrenaline of the fight had worn off, and his headache returned with greater force; Roger felt utterly exhausted and in a miserable state to complete his investigation and story. Peaches looked significantly worse off from his fight with the large man, but he wasn't letting it slow him. Roger thought that Peaches's injuries weren't serious enough for a hospital visit, and perhaps the Fountain Spring House would suffice. The two didn't speak much to each other for the rest of the walk. At a couple of points in time, Peaches and Roger would look over to each other with a smug grin that surfaced from such scrappy victories. Roger composed himself as best he could as he sighted the hotel down the street and said his farewell to Peaches, who was staying at the Fountain Inn at the corner of East and Broadway. It was just after two in the morning, and Roger heaved himself up the stairs to his hotel room. He took off his jacket and his shoes and crawled into bed after a day that proved immensely trying, but oddly satisfying.

2

When Roger woke up in the morning, he remembered dreaming about being back in the Fountain Spring House with a beautiful woman. Maybe it was Lucy. At least, he liked to think hers was the face of the woman that he already couldn't remember clearly. In the dream, the water grew too hot, and it began to look murky, and Roger felt pain in his hand. Then he woke up and wanted to go back to sleep knowing that nearly all of his work was ahead.

Roger had come back too late last night to arrange for his courtesy call and saw that the sunlight was already high and warm through his windows. His throat was scratchy, he still had a headache, and felt nauseous. He cleaned himself up as best he could under the circumstances and changed his shirt. To have any chance of coherent discourse with the professor, Roger decided he would eat first. He enjoyed a breakfast of sliced melon, vegetable hash, broiled veal cutlets, fried tomatoes, coffee, and apple juice. Roger had intended to be brief, merely to recuperate and settle his stomach. But as he picked at the last scraps of his food, he grew more comfortable and lingered much longer than he intended as sunbeams warmed the wood floor near his feet. He noticed the time—quarter-past ten. He hurried out, recalling the lapsed meeting time of either nine or nine-thirty, and attempted to justify his more leisurely meal knowing he would have been unable to make the meeting time in either case.

Roger eventually arrived at the Carroll College library. Although it was a Sunday, it was also mid-semester, and Linden arranged for them to meet here. Roger felt the unease of explaining his lateness and half-hoped that Professor Linden had dismissed himself from the appointment after a certain amount of waiting. The library was only open until one in the afternoon on Sundays, and when Roger made it inside the building he saw a couple of groups of students and one solitary fellow at a desk with a few books stacked next to him. The man was reading an older book and delicately turning one of the pages. He glanced up at Roger and then closed the book. "Just a minute, Mr. Merrick," the man said as he began gathering his materials. "You've kept me waiting for a little while now, so I don't suppose it would terribly inconvenience you while I pack up here?"

"Mr. Linden?" Roger spoke with too much agitation, which stemmed from continually being recognized by people he hadn't met yet. He noticed his tone and attempted to salvage the greeting. "I am extremely sorry, Mr. Linden . . . "

"No, you're not." The professor replied calmly and without spite, very carefully lowering the final book into his satchel as he rose and pushed in his chair.

"Mr. Linden, truly, I . . ."

"No, you're really not," he responded, still with no

hint of confrontation. "I am confident that you regret your embarrassment, and I would venture, since you seem like a nice enough fellow, maybe even the small loss of my time. But you're not 'extremely sorry.' We all lead our lives making decisions." He walked past Roger and toward the exit of the library, gesturing for Roger to follow. "We make these decisions in the moment, weighing the best or preferred option, and almost always seize that option. At times, we are pressed by obligations: professional or familial, and are coerced this way." They crossed through the main doors back into the crisp autumn air. Professor Linden abruptly stopped and lightly pressed his finger on Roger's sternum. "You, sir, made a decision that caused you to be late to our appointment." His face soured as he said these last words much more sternly. He now stared at Roger, waiting for a response.

"What you say is true of course, professor. But . . ."

"But nothing! That's simply the matter of it." Another brief but dragging silence followed, and then Linden smiled. "But don't think that I blame you for it! It's a past matter now." He finally withdrew his finger and clasped Roger on the shoulder. "I had a very productive morning. I don't think it could have gone better if you weren't running late. I insist that people say precisely what they mean. Words are so cheap nowadays. I am one voice in the wilderness trying to restore their worth. Would you be so kind as to join me at my home for the interview? I have an office on campus of course, but I've spent enough time here for the day as I'd like. It's a short walk from here, and I think we have a healthy number of interesting things to discuss, over tea as an added bonus. And, I invite you to call me Reginald."

"That works for me, Reginald." Roger then scurried after professor's brisk pace, and the two proceeded down the street in silence.

Reginald Linden stood at over six feet tall. He wore a royal maroon shirt, with a black tie and charcoal vest. His long hair was slicked back and tied into a ponytail. Roger concluded that he was either remarkably young for a full professor or was one of those unusually well-preserved fellows. His outfit and hairstyle would look absurd for most men and was aloof from the style of the age. Yet Roger decided that somehow this appearance translated to eccentric and even graceful for Reginald—a man unconcerned by fashion trends. He had a keen gaze and a sort of uncompromising, remarkably upright posture. Roger and Reginald walked south down East Avenue toward a neighborhood of tidily kept yards. Linden led them past a wrought iron gate to a door of solid oak—the entrance to an ornate and tasteful home of gray stone.

Inside of Reginald's home, he brought them into the study and excused himself to prepare the tea. It appeared that the professor lived alone and was doing comparatively well for himself. Roger wondered the status of the Linden family or if he had inherited any wealth. The walls of the study were almost all lined with completely stocked bookshelves, and as Roger scanned with his eyes, he saw that most were on various historical subjects, starting in the classical period through the mid-nineteenth century. A corner of the room sheltered from sunlight had shelves with books that looked exceptionally old and were behind glass. On Linden's desk were tall stacks of volumes on American Indian history and geography. Roger noticed a small side table next to the main leather office chair. On its surface was an exceptionally decrepit open book, displaying strange characters on the faded pages.

This tome piqued Roger's interest, who leaned over to look more closely. The text was completely unintelligible, the lines of characters were written in some honey-colored ink on a type of tanned leather pages. The script gently oscillated and waved, as if blowing in the breeze. Just looking at the characters caused Roger's headache to begin creeping back. There was some sort of grotesque illustration on the left page . . . a strange, anguished human face, as if screaming, its expression exacerbated by its missing eyes. Near the visage was the sketch of large arthropodan creature, its body looking something like a mutated tree trunk. Roger noticed that the book next to it was a handwritten attempt at a translation of the text, likely by Linden. "It'll be just a few more minutes!" Reginald called from another room. Possessed by an abrupt curiosity, Roger brought out his notepad and furiously copied the page that Reginald's translation was turned to, and observing that the professor had not yet returned, turned the translation to its previous page for more transcription. In his dexterous scribbling he did not think of the words' meaning. Indeed, he comprehended nothing in that moment; he gave all of his energies to copying quickly. As he heard footsteps, he turned the page back and darted back to his seat. Roger flipped his notepad to a fresh page just as Reginald, now wearing a burgundy-colored smoking jacket, returned with the tea. His host seemed to take no notice of any furtiveness and took his seat at his desk.

Reginald began with some small talk; he wished to avoid weighty topics while the tea was fresh. Reginald brought up Wisconsin's governor, Robert LaFollette, as a person of interest for Roger to follow in the next few years. He believed that a presidential bid would surface, perhaps in the '08 election. Roger conveyed to the professor that Waukesha was a charming town, filled with good-natured people, yet was frank about the various pressures he'd been under. Reginald acknowledged his familiarity with his troublesome new acquaintance.

"Bradley Evers . . . the administration of the college is friendly with him, probably hoping for another gift, or even a full Evers Automation grant one of these years. The man isn't inherently caustic, I've had a handful of pleasant interactions with him, but if he identifies a person or institution as an obstacle, he is both ruthless and unscrupulous. These industrialists often have to act this way to survive in their very competitive craft, I'm told. Still, that's horribly brutish, sending thugs after you. A poor reflection on our community. Do you plan to press charges?"

"I was thinking about filing a police report. I could positively identify one of the assailants, and I could probably pick out the other two if I had the opportunity," Roger replied, noticing that he had been rubbing his head where the scraggly fellow had struck him.

"You could," Reginald replied, sounding rather uninterested. "But I'm afraid your word won't win the day in court without corroborating testimonies." He then shifted in his chair and leaned forward, crossing his arms over his desk and looking at Roger more intently. "But you came to write mainly on the springs, yes?"

"Yes, I did. The Fountain Spring House is quite lovely indeed, but at this rate, it will likely phase out on its own accord, with or without my reports."

"Whether the fountain houses disappear is not of great concern to me," Reginald said, seamlessly intoning his bored voice. "I think they will always carry on in some capacity, on a smaller scale. But the fate of our community's natural springs and waterways are of importance, and most of the community seems to be missing the point. Too often we encroach on our natural resources and deal irreparable damage, only realizing once it's far too late. I've heard the argument that if the Spring House closes, the last bastion of commercial interest propping up our waterways against pollution would be removed. So in that sense, you can say I unofficially support them. Sam River appears to be the only other voice that I know especially concerned about the water sources themselves."

"I met an Indian gentleman named Sam," Roger offered.

"That is the same man. He throws excellent gatherings, too."

"Would you then describe yourself as a . . . what's the term? Conservationist?"

"Oh, like our dear president Mr. Roosevelt? I suppose, if you insist, you could mark me down as such. There are worse titles to be granted. People can call themselves anything, but the only labels that are worth anything are always self-apparent, self-demonstrated. I'll confess that I do hope his rumblings are more than just lip-service for preserving the great beauty of this nation's wild country . . . " As Roger looked up from his writing he noticed that Reginald's eyes had almost glazed over as he spoke these concluding lines. The professor was looking out into the yard beyond the one large window of the study, the wisp of steam still billowing from his tea, and a silence followed. The only delicate sounds were the blowing of the October wind and the motion of a grandfather clock's pendulum, near the foyer. As if returning from a dream, Reginald straightened in his chair and regarded Roger with a new focus. "I have some copies of some local history that I've been writing on the area. Please peruse them at your leisure, and reference and utilize anything that you see fit. It's not a finalized draft, but I am comfortable enough if you wish to quote me on anything."

Roger glanced at a manila folder, which had subsections labeled *Geography of the Fox River Waterway, History of Indigenous Peoples of the Waukesha Watershed,* and *Unexplained Mysteries: the Cultural Legends of the Waukesha Springs.* The last one seemed particularly interesting to Roger, and upon flipping open that section, he noticed the familiar term *Haunchyville*, from the *Freeman* article. Reginald had compiled a small article of his own on it. Suddenly, Roger noticed that Reginald had left his seat, still holding his tea, and was looking right over Roger's shoulder. *He can move like an absolute ghost when he wants to!* Roger thought, alarmed.

"Ah! Haunchyville! Horribly clumsy and uncouth name, but that seems to be sticking with the population at large," Reginald spoke with animation. "At first glance, it's one of those rather uninspired urban legends. A handful of people claim to see a village fashioned out of trees and natural structures for mythical dwarves. There's a funny bit about circus performers in one of its origins. I dismissed it, until the disappearance of a fellow who had briefly consulted with me on the matter, Mr. Eugene Shepard."

"Disappearance?" Roger shot back excitedly. "You mean to say he has been filed as missing? Wasn't he just interviewed by the *Freeman* but a month or so ago?"

"This is all true." Reginald removed his arm from the back of my chair and began pacing the room. " He discovered some of my academic interests in local history and geography. All that I was able to offer him is essentially all there in that folder," Reginald chuckled. "In fact, I had provided him that very same one, and you are fortunate that he returned it before his disappearance. I have no clue as to how much of it he actually read, however." Reginald smiled, but more mischievously than usual. "Are you called as an investigative journalist to look after Mr. Shepard's disappearance?"

"Well, I would hope that the local law enforcement

would be handling that!" Roger said, breathless at the wealth of leads and tangents the professor provided. "You are right though; all sorts of things are springing up now—no pun intended. It looks like I'm going to have quite a full platter, in any case."

"Indeed! I keep myself regularly preoccupied as well, but don't hesitate to come by if you wish to consult on anything else that you uncover. I daresay you have more initiative than any reporter for the *Freeman* that I've encountered; of course, you hail from a larger and more competitive outfit in Chicago. Were there any other specific questions that you had for me today, Roger?"

"I think we'll both be better served after I've properly perused your notes, Reginald. I'll be in touch if you don't mind doing a follow-up before I leave town. I do have the number now for your college office." Roger rose from his chair and collected his materials. "Take care, Professor, and thank you for the tea."

"And I encourage you to heed your advice too, Roger. I think your position takes on a good deal more trouble than mine, even danger, perhaps."

"Let us hope it does not come to that," Roger replied. The two exchanged a handshake, and Roger went off into the brisk autumn afternoon. He felt that he could sleep the moment he made it back to his hotel room and thought that not a half-bad idea, combined with reading the professor's notes. His headache was gone, but his back ached, and he felt fatigued. As Roger looked at Reginald's notes he decided to avoid looking at his secretive copy of the strange translation for the moment and began by taking a cursory look at the *Geography of the Fox River Waterway*. Earlier Roger had obtained a county map dated from 1891 that detailed the land ownership of the various plots outside of the town proper. Roger wondered how much had changed since this was drawn up. Sam River's name was missing from this version, which was odd, as Roger recalled the property being acquired in the 1870s. At any rate, it would be useful to know whose land he would be entering, were he to take more of a foray into the wider country.

There was no appearance of the mysterious Haunchyville on any map of course, but Roger's mind already began to drift to the idea that somewhere in this terrain there could be little wonders, tucked away. There was a considerable mix of marsh and woodlands that were being systematically cleared by the growing population of the town. The next file on the *History of Indigenous Peoples* of the area began with sources of Jean Nicolet, the earliest European explorer of Wisconsin. The Ho-Chunk Indians were the primary group of the area, and there followed a long history of disease outbreaks alongside territorial struggle—defending their territory in wars and skirmishes with the Potawatomi and Menominee Indians and later with the French and English colonial powers. Linden cited historian Francis Parkman the most frequently, although had a final section that was drawn primarily from his research and interviews in the area. This section described a "lost tribe" near Waukesha that went extinct in the early 1800s, whose proper name, according to Linden, has been forgotten.

This "lost tribe" inhabited the area of Waukesha before the first wave of European settlement in the area during the mid-1830s, and Linden speculated that they were not an offshoot of the Ho-Chunk but originated from another place. Linden's summation of the group suggested that they had many unique characteristics of groups in the area, including an alphabetical writing system and esoteric religion. There were even examples of some of the characters of the lost tribe's language which were argued to reflect the importance of flowing water, or perhaps long roots, in their stretched calligraphy. Roger's thoughts drifted back to the strange script he saw in Linden's office. Linden's style was compelling, and his claims were sensational, but the sources on the lost tribe were so thin that Roger was not surprised that Linden had not propelled himself to any fame or elite position out east. The conclusion of the section argued that the Waukesha springs were centers of religious ceremonies. By the end of this section, Roger had grown hungry and distracted, but he was determined that he would finish at least skimming the folder before going down to dinner.

Roger rubbed his forehead at these notes, hoping that the last section, *Unexplained Mysteries and Cultural Legends of the Waukesha Springs,* which he had reserved for last, would at least prove interesting as his outlook grew bleaker. He went straight to the section on the increasingly curious "Haunchyville." Linden did his best to sort through conflicting stories about circus dwarves, cannibalism, Old Scratch as an albino man who haunted and protected the village, and dozens of proposed locations of the village. Consistencies in the story featured a forested enclave of miniature hovels hewn from the wood of the nearby trees, inhabited by dwarves. Linden's bemusement was evident as he commented on the various origins of the myth, which he ultimately ascribed to the creativity of a local farmstead which then spread to the town, in time.

The remainder of the *Legends* section described some of the springs functioning as portals to distance places, one of the springs being the Fountain of Youth, a spawning pool for the infamous Bigfoot, and a farmer's ghost known as Tobias Bushell who haunted the cornfields in the area in the late moons of autumn before the first snowfall. There was a scribbled caption, apparently a joke from Linden that suggested that one of the mysterious moons of Jupiter could be accessed through the portal of a spring cave. There was ultimately nothing of great importance to Roger, but at the very least he did not regret discovering some of the layers of folklore. Roger could infuse some of the details and had a productive first meeting with Linden, but he felt he would need perhaps another one or two quality perspectives to constitute a full article although his report still lacked a spark.

Roger decided to take an early dinner, consisting of broiled chicken, baked sweet potatoes, cauliflower, plum sauce, cabbage salad, and peach pyramid. As he finished his plate, he once again saw his friend Peaches, who was still recovering. Peaches offered a seemingly half-serious (at least, Roger hoped) invitation to go out on the town that night, but then reminded Roger of Sam River's summons to his property this evening. Roger was amazed that Peaches remembered that interaction from McGinty's, who seemed to retain his memory very well amidst drinking. The two kept their conversation short as Roger checked with Peaches to see if he was going too. Peaches still appeared to be having a hard time understanding what exactly the event was, and to his credit, Roger wasn't feeling sharp about his explanation. Roger then scrambled back to his room to ready himself for the powwow.

Roger was a tad unsure of what to wear for an occasion such as this but favored the straightforward approach of being suitably warm enough for the Wisconsin fall season. Roger donned his jacket with his less formal pants, a heavy scarf that would cover his neck and part of his ears, and a plaid patterned newsboy hat, one of three that he had packed. He had a few minutes remaining and remembered his translation of the strange, tattered book from Reginald's desk. He flipped back in his notepad and tore out those pages, setting them down on his reading table. A short note from Reginald introduced a passage on an entity known as Ta'halmuk, or "Thalmak" as Reginald preferred to phonetically render it. Roger began reading from the first page:

And it is within the transcendence of flowing waters, the bosom of thought, that I, X'arta, heard the echoing call of the steward of the land, the great lord below. And he is a great son opposed to the great daughter, whose offspring are many. But he is one scorned, abhorrent to his kin, faceless, and his name is Thalmak, the Whispering Root of one hundred thousand miles. He makes his dwelling beneath the land, alike to it but alien. He dreams harshly as the land cries out, he succors to no end the hunger of the cracked surface and the scathing wind. To alter essence as Thalmak does, to consume, to exist, to gain mastery over old things, there is nothing else for a vessel to aspire. Consecrate your understanding and proscribe all else. Graft your essence, and become changed, as he changes even the dark young, and moves the very plates of the Earth, far beneath. Learn from his flesh, which draws power from the primordial earth. Apart from this lifeblood, there is naught but void. This world is darkness, and here is found remedy . . .

The "remedy" that followed was something of a ritual. Even translated by Reginald's hand, the description made not the slightest bit of sense to Roger. There were gruesome preparations involving a gesture of self-mutilation and drinking of a strange milk, chanting, burying personal trinkets in specific geometric patterns, at certain sacred grounds. A separate ritual involved the infusion of fresh human blood into various waterways to reinvigorate the land's fertility. *What on earth is the basis that professor uses for a completely unknown script? Was this translation a reflection of Reginald's own darker tendencies?* Roger had seen a few foreign language books when scanning the bookshelves of Reginald's study, but still had difficulty with the idea as to how reliable Reginald's translation would prove. Even still,

Roger could not help but feeling a small pang of morbid curiosity regarding the rest of the text. A strange thought, almost a compulsion sprung up to seek it out, but Roger quelled this, as he was pressed by calling appointments.

3

Down in the lobby, Roger once again saw Peaches, along with Ms. Lucy. Roger immediately took off his hat in greeting and couldn't help but smile at the refreshing change of company compared to his notes and macabre readings. Peaches stepped forward. "I may have let slip at the Spring House that you were attending Sam's little party. Turns out, Ms. Morris has been known to attend on occasion, and was in need of an escort!"

"Not *in need* of an escort, Mr. Graham!" Lucy gently corrected. "And you really do need to leave poor Cynthia alone before she leaves her fiancé for you!" Peaches blushed and turned his head down, muttering a vague defense. "But I do prefer having a good companion for such social affairs." She resumed, lighting up the entire lobby with her smile. "I hope you do not object, Mr. Merrick?"

"It would be my honor, Ms. Lucy! Errm, Ms. Morris . . ."

"Lucy is preferable, Mr. Merrick," Lucy responded as she took Roger's left arm as the two left the hotel. Roger gave a final, appreciative nod to Peaches, who just winked at him as best he could through his swollen eye.

"Then I would ask that you please call me Roger." He

could feel her drawing closer as a gust hit them right as they rounded the corner down the street. Earlier that day Roger had arranged for a coach to take him out to Sam's, and it had arrived right on time. The two stepped into the carriage, which was empty, although the carriage driver mentioned something about grabbing a couple of others on the trip out to Sam's. Roger closed the door and sat across from his date, weighing his mind on how to best make use of this time in private with Lucy as the carriage began along the street.

"What the devil did you and that Peaches fellow get into last night?" Lucy began, touching near a bruise on Roger's face with the backs of her fingertips, not masking her concern.

"We got into some . . . rough stuff with some henchmen, I suppose you could call them. That Bradley Evers fellow's way of sending a message. The most foolish thing about it is that I hadn't even really said much in the way of confrontation, but he seems to have made up his mind about me now."

"Your friend Peaches came to the Spring House again today. He stayed in a pool a full twenty minutes beyond what we normally permit, but I didn't have the heart to expel him. Normally I don't hesitate with such things, but we rarely have such battered guests. You don't look so bad," she added, scanning Roger as best she could, "although I haven't gotten as full of a view of you as with Peaches."

"Well I'd be happy to provide you with one!" Roger replied, earnestly. "At the Spring House, of course," he added.

"I don't know why you thought that needed clarification!"

Lucy replied, and turned her head to the side, flustered by the clumsy dalliance of her carriage-mate, while also trying to make out whether it was intentional. "Your friend was swollen up in quite a few places," she resumed. "It's a small wonder he made it in this morning without you guiding him down the street."

"He's a resilient guy. A bit, um, simple, but a good friend to have in a pinch, as it turned out. It's been interesting keeping company with a ballplayer."

"Have you gathered all of your information that you needed? I suppose any day now it's back on the train to, what is it, the Union Depot in Chicago?"

"Nearly there, but I have another couple of days. And really, I didn't mean to upset you the other morning!"

"It's all right," Lucy replied somewhat vacantly, now looking out the window as the carriage. "It's just hard enough running a business as a woman. My father was an investing partner in the Spring House. Three daughters in the Morris household, no boys. I took to the trade, and I've loved working there. But I hadn't anticipated a Chicago journalist coming by for my list of challenges this month."

"I am not your adversary," Roger replied, leaning forward, eyes widened. "The *Tribune*, I'm . . . trying to determine what to make of the whole situation down there. I only wanted to provide you the opportunity to give your perspective.

"I know. You're probably right too, about the Springs," she said with an abrupt air of resignation. "I don't think that you'll find any one person who knows the reason why people aren't returning to the Springs as much anymore. But there are some who won't have trouble fitting it in their narrative. 'An establishment folds under the management of a woman,'" she said swinging her head in a deeper, didactic tone.

"Well, you aren't out of business just yet. You'll have at least one returning customer coming in before the week is out! I am also of the opinion that if anyone can find a way to keep a business alive, it would be you!"

"That's very sweet of you," Lucy said, with a small smile. "But what makes you say something like that? Journalists need evidence, don't they?"

"I . . . I say that because I think you have a strong spirit. Indomitable is the word. There's a certain strength in the way you speak, your uncompromising frankness, that keen, beautiful light in your eyes when you confront unpleasant truths. And you seem like the kind of person who will do everything possible to change them. I'd like to say I'm becoming fairly comfortable around people, in my line of work. But I keep finding that I'm a bit of a mess when in your company, and I can't decide if it's more from your wit, or how gorgeous you are, Ms. Lucy Morris!"

"You haven't started your drinking this early with your friend Peaches, have you?" Before Roger could answer, Lucy spoke again, very softly, "I'm teasing. That was a Pulitzer-winning answer Roger Merrick," now also beginning to lean towards Roger, who felt his gravity now shifting to her, their eyes locked together. "You talk very sweet, for someone being in a mess . . . "

"Good evening!" An older woman said as the door of the carriage flung open with a rush of cold air. She stepped in, dressed very finely wearing a hat with an unhealthy-looking pressed flower in it, and greeted them. "Cooler weather we've been having, but at least it's been staying dry! My name is Jessica, Jessica Pickett. I hope the two of you aren't bound for Sam River's residence!"

Roger looked back at Lucy, both mirroring a wounded expression yielding eventually to resigned bemusement at the fateful interruption. A man stepped in after Jessica Pickett. He was of similar age, perhaps he was Mr. Pickett. His cheeks and ears were bright red from the cold, and he regarded Roger and Lucy with a nod. The pair both slid in next to Lucy, who, to Roger's delight, scooted over across his side to balance the cabin.

"Oh, you did not need to move, dear! Bruce, you should have just plopped down next to that gentlemen there." Bruce gave something of an apologetic grumble, then leaned his head back and shut his eyes. Jessica Pickett sat like a rigid board, although she still had a small hunch, and folded her hands in her lap, looking at Roger. "So, you were saying . . . where you were taking the carriage this evening?

"Oh, right. Well, I'm Roger Merrick for the *Chicago Tribune*, and perhaps you know Ms. Lucy Morris of the Fountain Spring House? I'm afraid um… Mrs. Pickett, is it?" The older woman nodded, intently. "I'm afraid that we are in fact, on our way to Sam River's, although I don't suppose you'd say why you'd have a problem with this?"

"Damn racket!" Bruce piped in, without opening his eyes.

"Well, we are his neighbors." Mrs. Pickett began. "We take the same carriage that many of his guests do on our way back from church, brunch, and our other Sunday engagements. These . . . powwows are often at night, and we don't object to bonfires or gatherings, but there is often alcohol at these events. As a member of the area's temperance league, I can't say that I am in support of that. Don't give me that look. I know how much of an uphill battle it is in this state! But just like our struggle for the vote," she said with a glance to Lucy, "it's still worth fighting for. But what's more, we've . . . noticed that many of the people who show up at these parties never bother to attend church on Sundays!"

"Mrs. Pickett, perhaps they simply aren't members of your congregation?" Roger offered.

"Certainly not! We are certain that they aren't showing up at any legitimate worship service. We have league members from practically all denominations in the area . . . we even have a Catholic! You seem like nice enough people. Are you sure you want to get mixed up with that crowd?"

"I'm afraid that my line of work leads me to mixing in with all types of people. But I'll tell you, Mrs. Pickett, he was perfectly friendly with me, and he seems a very community-minded man."

"Well, I suppose if it's for your professional duties . . . but I can't imagine you'll get too much information of worth." She produced a handkerchief and blew her nose several times.

Roger waited politely for this to finish but did not want

to leave the conversation there. "Well, I know of a professor who has attended at least one in the past. But I—"

"Oh, you mean that Linden!" Mrs. Pickett interrupted. "He's the worst out of them all! A Freemason, or worse! Probably belongs to some secret society that I couldn't even begin to describe, nor would I want to!" A silence followed, with only the clopping hooves of the horses along the street perforating the air. "And you've seen his . . . appearance! What kind of man looks like that?" She paused, perhaps waiting for some form of agreement on the part of the younger people, but pressed on after the silence. "Well, it seems like you may be a lost cause, although you seem nice enough," Mrs. Picket smiled as she patted Roger on the shoulder. "But if you heed anything that I've said, just steer clear of . . . Reginald Linden!" She finished with some difficulty as if it the name left a bad taste in her mouth.

The rest of the carriage ride passed by without incident or much talking. Roger ventured a question about the Spring House, which Ms. Pickett replied to have visited at one time, but found the overall atmosphere like something of Babylon. This closing remark effectively sucked the air out of the cabin, and Bruce had indicated that he was not one for conversation. Roger wouldn't have given much thought to the busybody's words about the professor had he not looked at that strange translation. His mind was now a bit divided about what, exactly, to make of the professor, but Roger remained confident his next interaction with the man himself would clear up any uncertainties. The two pairs were dropped off at the meeting point of the properties, and Roger put his arm around Lucy's shoulder as they braced themselves from the assault of a northerly wind. It wasn't hard to see the small crowd organized in a circle near a charming farmhouse on a wide plot of land. Roger saw Sam and about a dozen others in ceremonial dress. A few were manning some large drums, and the others were in the center circle, rhythmically dancing and proceeding to the beat of the drums. The dancers occasionally and variably sang out. Some of the attendees clearly had Native American ancestry, who mingled with other attendees from the town. Roger sat down over by a familiar face, Reginald Linden.

"You've brought some very charming company, Roger!" Linden rose to greet the pair, dressed in a gray overcoat and extending a gloved handshake. (His other hand held a flask.) "A pleasant coincidence running into you here. I believe the powwow has officially started.. You could share some Ho-Chunk culture with your readers in a snippet, perhaps?" Reginald turned to Lucy. "You look familiar, miss."

"Do I? Well, I'm Lucy Morris, and I manage the Fountain Spring House."

"That's it. No one's a true stranger when living in Waukesha for a few years! Reginald Linden, of Carroll College.

"Oh, we've just got an earful about you on the carriage over here, Mr. Linden. You've got a way of terrorizing the older ladies of the community, you know?"

Reginald waived a hand in dismissal. "You should

understand better than most, Ms. Lucy, that when you give yourself to your work, family-minded or traditional people may voice their displeasure or disappointment. There is no nosier creature in the universe than an old shrew, and the most interesting observations that they have are their imagined ones." He was speaking calmly, although Roger perceived some agitation in his bearing compared to earlier in the day. "Best not to chat too much right now, in due courtesy to the powwow. There will be time soon enough."

Roger enjoyed the powwow, although he found difficulty articulating the reasons. There was something serene and yet energizing about the sounds and dance. The weather conditions had turned mild for that time of year, reducing Roger's shivering, he took comfort in his company. The ceremony evoked an ageless facet of the natural world in its outdoor setting, and although Roger could not interpret the words of the chanting song, he felt welcome. Roger's mind drifted towards questions of the way society partitioned the land and pushed back the people and communities that were here before. Thoughts of the Ho-Chunk, the lost tribe, the Germans, the Irish, the great challenges to the communal aspect of souls spending a brief while on this area of the country, on this very terra. *We brace ourselves from the want and harshness of the Earth's climate, the long winters. But we also owe our survival to that same harshness that yields to warmth and plenty in its own time. How much the same is it, among our interactions with each other?* When Roger sat down at the beginning of the powwow, his mind wandered between his current assignment, thoughts of Lucy, that infernal book and the shadowy professor, fears of thugs in alleys, and lurking creatures in derelict forests. Now, his mind was clear, and he decided he would do everything he could in his writings to bolster the Spring House.

When the powwow ended, some left but most of the guests and participants remained as a great bonfire, which had been kindled during the powwow, swelled and roared to fill the large pit. Sam came over and warmly greeted Roger and the others, thanking them for their attendance and offering some libations, cheese, nuts, berries, and meat that he brought out on three great wood platters for his guests. "It's very much a Wisconsin platter for this season although I've preserved a number of the berries from my bushes from this summer," Sam said, making his rounds. The talking was light-hearted, and Roger was surprised by Reginald, who laughed and jested much more freely than his eccentric sharpness from earlier in the day. Roger refrained from drinking nearly as much as he did last evening, finding that his stomach protested more quickly this evening. Roger wanted to find out a few things before the pleasant night ended. "When can the world expect your monograph on the lost tribe of the Waukesha watershed, Reginald?"

"Oh, that would never get published by an academic press," Reginald raised a hand, dismissively, "at least, not with my current . . . materials. Something else would have to be unearthed. My next book will be more grounded than that."

"Some of those old tomes in your office . . . any writings from the lost tribe?" Roger asked, carefully.

"That's an appointment for another time, Mr. Merrick," replied the professor, with some relish.

"Fine, be furtive if you wish, but truly, are you a member of some secret society? Mrs. Pickett has buzzed in my ear, and I won't be denied!" Roger persisted, enjoying putting the formidable man on the spot.

"I'm afraid I am not, although I have half a mind to form one—maybe a Wisconsin conservationist's league if you'd care to join me as founding members?" he asked, gesturing to include Lucy. Roger turned to see Sam, who had found a seat next to the group.

"I'm watching you closely, Mr. Merrick," Sam said sternly, which quickly gave way to a smile. "Although I'm not nearly as worried about cutting off your drink when you're not in the company of your friend Peaches. How's the story coming along?"

"I'm doing a rather poor job of writing it. I must be seeking out too many adventures."

"Hah! Then you're doing an excellent job bringing out the adventure in this place yourself! Waukesha isn't exactly known for its excitement. Save when a few rough types used to come around terrorizing my gatherings." His tone shifted, and a shadow had fallen on across his face, which shifted in the dancing firelight. "Although that hasn't been for over a year, thanks mainly to the company of some of my more distinguished guests," with a glance over to Reginald.

"You see that Sam is the consummate gentleman," Reginald quipped. "Generous as a host and gracious with his praise," he added, rising to his feet. "I take my leave; I teach class in the morning, after all. Good night to you all! Perhaps our paths will cross once more before you return to Chicago, Roger? And a great pleasure, Ms. Morris."

Sam took the seat vacated by Reginald. It was growing late, and as the hour wore on, less care was being taken to stoke the fire as it slowly dwindled. Most of the guests had returned home and Roger asked Sam about the "rough types" he had mentioned. From the gist of it, some fellows had come by with shotguns on two occasions, shouting insults and vulgarities. No one had been hurt; it was only a bristling display with some shots at windows or into the air. It had been enough to discourage Sam from organizing the gatherings until he received the backing of Reginald Linden as a guest. Sam insisted the professor was part of some powerful circle and was far humbler in person, though he did not know the source of his influence or why he chose to reside in a relatively small midwestern town.

"I would think he would be in Milwaukee at least, or Chicago. Also, doesn't the name sound English? I never did find out if he's a European, his accent isn't Midwestern. I've always wagered he's connected to the Illuminati, because came out of Europe," Sam remarked lightly. "There's an odd colleague of his at Carroll, Travis Dillard; he always likes to talk about them. But Mr. Reginald also has more sense than most seeing the way industry has a way of tearing up the earth around it, like with that damn Evers and his mills. We've spoken about the issue, and he's promised we'll win the argument sooner rather than later. Truly, a great man . . ." Sam's voice trailed off as he stared at the dying fire.

"Oh, well the location detail should be easy Sam. The professor wants to be close to his research, his lost tribe." Roger paused suddenly as Lucy's head had dipped on to his shoulder, her eyes closed.

"If there really is a lost tribe, it could make the territorial disputes even more confusing around here." Sam noticed Lucy's head perched on Roger's shoulder. "Looks like it's going to be even more difficult for you to leave our town now," Sam said gently.

"I'm not sure how I'll manage it, to be honest," Roger sighed. "Just when something starts becoming clear, I find some other distraction, pleasant or otherwise. I'm going to need to take things one day at a time."

Sam mentioned that he had arranged for one more carriage to come by. It would be the last opportunity to return, save spending the evening in a larger room in his house with a couple other guests. Sam had two children, both living elsewhere, and his wife had succumbed to consumption several years ago, and he did not mind having overnight company. Roger thanked Sam but roused Lucy to return downtown. The return back was in tired silence. Lucy seemed adept at catching pockets of sleep. Roger looked out the frosted carriage window and saw a strange light in the sky over a patch of woods to the west. It was a dim light, not even as candescent as that of a full moon's, but it was of a strange hue. Shades of washed-out orange, crimson, and purple danced in a waving gradient along the tops of the trees, resonating in the faint aura in the sky above.

Roger decided that he was too tired and had heard somewhere that it was possible to experience hallucinations when this sleep-deprived. That, or he was looking at some astral ceremony above Haunchyville, perhaps. The thought made him chuckle. Indeed, he had been running on too little rest all day. When the carriage arrived back at the corner of East and Main Street, his insistence on walking Lucy home was rebutted thoroughly.

"It's just a few blocks down," Lucy began. "It's something I'm perfectly comfortable with. Think about it, I wouldn't be able to run a business if I can't take a few walks in Waukesha at night. Besides, you also shouldn't be offering to walk me home when you aren't going to be sticking around. How would I go anywhere once you're gone?"

Roger could not muster the energy to protest any longer, although Lucy didn't seem to mind his attempt. She swept in and gave Roger a delicate kiss on the cheek and embraced him. He could feel the warmth of her body as she lingered there. "Why aren't there more men like you around here?" she said, softly.

Then Lucy pulled back a little, still loosely in Roger's arms which were lightly clasped on her shoulders. He had a response ready but persevered against his swift instincts as a journalist. The two exchanged small smiles and savored the moment of contentment. "I would ask why there aren't more women like you in Chicago, but that wouldn't convey my meaning." Lucy laughed at that. "Since you refused my walk home, perhaps you'd spare me one more kiss?" The two grew ever closer.

Roger stood in the hallway outside of his room. He had worn a drowsy smile since he at last parted with Lucy, as they had arranged a date for tomorrow night. A door closed in some distant hallway or floor, and Roger stretched out his hand towards the door handle. He became alarmed as it yielded, creaking forward since it had already been open just a crack. Quite sure that he had locked the door of the room before heading down to dinner, Roger rapidly considered his options. He decided he was too tired to return with the appropriate authorities and wagered naively that the intruder was either gone or not his match if he could surprise them. He would never have been so cavalier, but his tussle from the other night caused him to swell with a degree of unfounded confidence.

It appeared that the former was true as Roger peered into the dim lit room; whoever had broken in was long gone. Upon lighting the lamp, there was little disturbance that Roger could notice apart from the breached door. His papers looked a bit out of order, along with Reginald's loaned folder, but the two torn pages from his notebook with the strange translation were missing. Also, Roger's only finished article, a playful piece on Haunchyville, had been taken. Acknowledging the pain in rewriting that story, he hoped that either the success or disappointment of whoever had broken in was enough to keep them from returning, at least this night. He closed the door, although it would not properly latch without some repair. He took the chair of the small writing desk in the room and wedged it under the handle. *Let's hope housekeeping doesn't make an early call.* Roger readied himself for bed and then slept like the dead.

Roger did not dream, waking refreshed but regretting that he had missed the window for breakfast. Alas, it appeared that nothing could now save him from beginning the draft of his article. Roger removed the chair from underneath the door and got to work. Subsequently it creaked back and forth whenever a draft of air disturbed it, which brought Roger unexpected amusement. After about two hours of formulating his story and infusing it with quotations and details from his interviews, Roger sought refuge in a lunch break. Upon finishing his last morsels and observing the leanness of his wallet, he phoned Lou Baker.

"An extension through Friday? What the hell for?" Lou's voice barked through the receiver. "I can't put a story like this in 'The Sunday,' and I can't imagine it could be that complicated. You do know this was supposed to be for this Thursday's edition. Even if you got, say, four side stories from this . . . that's hardly worth an extension."

"I'm sure that's how it must seem sir, but you're going to have to—"

"It looks like you need a reminder about how this works, Merrick. You don't get to set the terms here like an army captain on the Oregon Trail after getting one out-of-town assignment. You're back in the office this Wednesday, by noon. End of negotiations."

Roger could hear Lou lingering on the end of the line as if waiting for a defiant remark from his reporter. None came, and there was a noted softening in his tone as he spoke again. "If you get this distracted on every out-of-town assignment Roger, you'll be doing puff-pieces and sports stories until you've got about as much hair as I do. It's for your own development, because believe it or not, I'm doing my best to look out for you, you ungrateful bastard!" His final remarks were meant as a jive, and despite Roger's disappointment, he chuckled.

"All right Lou, you got it. Say, there's a Cubs player down here as well, a Mr. Peaches Graham. I confess that I am not up to date on my baseball players . . ."

"Peaches Graham? I've got Scott here, so just a moment." There was about a minute's pause. "Peaches Graham . . . he pitched one game this season, and it was a loss. 'Cubs player' might be a little generous of a term for him, I'd say. No need for you to do any sports pieces!"

As Roger placed the receiver back down, he felt sufficiently cowed by his unflinching superior and calculated his remaining time. He had about two full days left in town, which was certainly time enough for finishing his articles. *Home stretch. Just a matter of procedure, really. Back to Chicago, back home . . .*

Roger returned to his table, and to a slice of desert and

a coffee freshly arrived. He was unaware that he was being monitored for quite some time while down in the lobby. The observer was unable to restrain himself any longer. He moved over to Roger's table slowly in an awkward shuffle while Roger remained in complete oblivion. Standing a few feet from Roger's table, the individual cleared his throat, twice, in an effort to get the journalist's attention, who continued sipping his coffee. Finally, Roger was startled as the an unkempt tramp plopped down in the chair across the table from him. Roger beheld a haggard, large man, wearing an oversized bowler. There was something vaguely familiar about him, but Roger couldn't place his face. He gave the man every opportunity to speak first, but the stranger hesitated, stuttering and starting over multiple times. In an instant, the glimpse of the man's face suddenly clicked in Roger's memory. It had been in an alley, attached to a body holding a knife.

"Good Christ, you're that hooligan from the alley!" Roger practically shrieked.

"Not so loud, please!" He pressed his hands down on Roger's forearms as he saw him about to mouth another exhortation. Several people were now looking over to their table. "Please! Damn it, if I really had it out for you, I wouldn't be sitting down to luncheon, would I?" Roger was unsatisfied, and about to hail an attendant. "You'll get us both thrown in jail!"

Roger breathed deeply, acknowledging the elementary truth of that, at least. "All right, fine. But for God's sake, you tried to kill my friend. And me!"

"Hah! Kill you? Oh, the knife?" The man produced one on the spot, observing Roger's reaction before putting it away. "I don't brawl without a knife. But if I wanted to kill you, I would have brought a shotgun!" He laughed coarsely, as if the quip brushed aside the matter like an old disagreement among friends.

"What on earth could you want now, then, if you're not here on behalf of Mr. Evers?"

"Evers? Pah, you've got me all wrong there. I ain't Evers's man. I'd like to say I'm my own." The man's eyes drifted to the half-eaten piece of cake on the table. "Are you going to be eating that?" He grinned as Roger silently pushed the plate closer to him. "Obliged. Shouldn't let it go to waste." His maw opened to receive the piece in one bite. "Name's Tom Moss. Evers wanted you roughed up, and that was the whole arrangement. But we didn't know you'd have that one brute with you. You ought not tell him—Evers—that I mentioned that though, or else we really might have a problem." Roger was proud of his ability to discern Moss's speech through his vigorous chewing, putting aside any disgust at the profound break in table manner.

"Very well, but you still haven't said why you're sitting here now."

"Oh, right! Ehem, well, I found out a bit after the fact that you're a reporter. I'd uh, like to sell you the rights to a story. It'd be a nice executive. No! A nice . . . exclusive for you? Ha, hahaha!"

"What kind of story, Mr. Moss? I'm afraid that we can't

dance around too much. My time left in town is dwindling, and I'm not necessarily inclined to you, you understand?"

"Oh, I understand all right, but I'm no fool. I can tell you this—it involves a missing person and a bit of a local legend, you might say. That's all I'm willing to divest, um, divulge. If you want the dirty details, I'll be glad to tell you for fifty dollars."

For the first time in the conversation, it was Roger's turn to have a small laugh. He was beginning to know the kind of man Moss, who had lost much of his aura of mystery and menace, was. Roger now perceived a man, perhaps hard on his times, looking to turn a dollar. He had never really met a true drifter, although that term might not apply to Moss since he seemed rooted in the area like a perennial weed. "Well, Mr. Moss, your price is rather steep for a tip-off, and I don't believe I'd like to add consorting with criminals and vagabonds to my resume," these last lines spoken as softly as possible to assuage his unpredictable contact. Roger may have well accepted in other circumstances, and if he had the money.

"A counteroffer, then?" Moss replied too quickly, suggesting desperation. Roger simply shook his head at the man. "Suit yourself. Might want to see about getting that lock fixed on your door," he rasped, a fiendish grin on his face as he started out of his chair.

"So that was you? Thanks for straightening that out!" Roger's words had checked Moss's movement from his seat. "Looks like you didn't find much worth stealing up there, huh?"

"I'm not saying that was me or not, but you should count yourself damned lucky that you're still—"

"Still what?" Roger interrupted, his patience now overspent on the tramp.

"Who's to say, really? I suppose I've taken enough of your time." Moss finally rose from his chair, then looked distractedly across the room, perhaps at someone. "But when you come back deciding that you want the story, it'll be seventy, and no haggling then. You need to have a better sense of opportunity, Roger Merrick." Moss excused himself from the table, and Roger exhaled.

Back in his room, Roger worked as best he could on the article on the Springs while an employee worked on the door in the hallway. "A momentary fumble where I thudded against the door when the key slipped . . . I believe I had enjoyed as much drink as was good for me," Roger had explained to the front desk staff, who glared at him and charged him in advance for the maintenance work. At any rate, Roger completed his first set of drafts. He read through his main story and saw that it was reminiscent of an advertisement, calling on people to return *en masse* to Waukesha and the Fountain Spring House. It dismissed the previous death as unconnected to the quality and practices of the Spring House, a fair defense as Roger had certainly found nothing to suggest a link. The story was only lightly tempered by some of the more balanced perspectives from individuals such as Linden. It would need a round of editing, but the decisive direction helped provide one of the more compelling tones that Roger believed he had put to paper. He wondered if the professor would still be in his office at Carroll College and decided he would make a visit before his date with Lucy. It seemed there was no great mystery after all to the decline of the Springs House, and Roger would save it, if he could.

4

Roger navigated the corridor of Main Hall until he found the long hallway which accommodated the faculty offices. There were less than a dozen, and as Roger scanned the panels outside of the doors, he noted the various programs of Classics, French, History, Geography, and Bookkeeping. Several of the professors were also ministers of the Presbyterian Church. He reached Reginald Linden's door, which was ajar, and found that the professor was engaged in a discussion with two of his colleagues. Reginald's face looked exhausted, but it had not deterred the lively oration of one of his guests. Reginald noticed Roger and gave him a slight nod, and the other gentlemen turned and acknowledged his presence, but then promptly resumed their discussion. As Roger remained in the doorway, he came to understand the conversation was about the Colonial Press's most recent edition of the *Decisive Battles of the World* by Sir Edward Shepherd Creasy. Roger had heard of the book before, and the animus of the debate in the professor's office centered on which battles were considered most important, both in the original text, and battles from the nineteenth century added by John Speed in 1889.

"Creasy loved the grand legacy of the European

Kingdoms," an older man said, who sat in a large leather-backed chair, facing Reginald, and had been talking for the better part of the last three minutes. He was plump, with a balding head that supported a remaining crop of silver hair on the back, and a fine plume of smoke rose from a pipe nestled in his hand. "But I don't think he was overfond of Catholics; otherwise, he would have included the action of the Knights of St. John at the Great Siege of Malta! But surely, Reginald, Travis, you must agree that the Battle of Yarmouk is his most egregious exclusion. Come now, a massive Byzantine coalition smashed by the Arab forces a mere fraction of the size? The whole faith of Islam lived or died on the chance of that swirling sandstorm on that battlefield!"

"I'm not a military historian," Reginald said in a tone that suggested he had already stated this fact a number of times. "I'm only remotely familiar with the Saratoga campaign."

"David," the other man said, who must have been Travis. He was closer of age to Reginald and slight of stature. His head was fully shaved, but he had a thin beard that was pristinely groomed. "We were supposed to focus the conversation on Speed's additions. But it's already nearly five o'clock, and like always, you go off chasing cataphracts and galleys instead of Gettysburg or the War with the Spaniards!"

"You are right," David responded, begrudgingly. "It must be tedium for you modernists to hear me to discuss the more glorious, ancient wars. *Tempus fugit*, and all that. But can it even be called history if happened within fifty years ago? I thought it was almost . . . arrogance on Speed's part to throw those in there. We still need to get the long perspective of their significance."

"The Civil War will prove tremendously important in the long-term—that's already been established," Travis added. "But goodness, here sits poor Reginald, putting up with another unraveled discourse. I think that's all for today, gentlemen. At least for me." Travis rose from his chair, which prompted David to do the same. They both put on their hats and stepped out into the hallway, where Roger still lingered. David scooped up a book with green binding, titled *The Rubaiyat of Omar Khayyam* in his arm, and offered a quick "G'evening" as he waddled down the hallway. Conversely, the other man offered a full introduction. "Travis Dillard, professor of History and French, Carroll College."

Roger introduced himself, and the two carried on for a moment outside of Reginald's office, who had a few things to finish up in the now precious quiet of his office. Travis provided an answer to Roger's question as to what a *cataphract* was: a heavily-armored cavalry soldier employed by the Byzantines and their Near-Eastern opponents alike. Dillard had been a member of the faculty for eleven years, and Roger presumed their conversation would be limited to pleasantries when he ventured a quick question. "Professor, you wouldn't happen to be a member of any external organizations, along with Reginald, by any chance?" Roger closed his notebook, conveying that this would be off the record. "I've heard a few things in town and wondered if you'd enlighten me?"

"I suppose it's no harm to tell you that I am a member

of a little group called the Astral Yeomen. I maintain it's healthy for an educated man to explore the new spiritualism. Reginald once was as well, but he resigned a little more than a year ago. Membership is available to town residents through invitation only," he said, while checking his pocket watch. "If you'll excuse me."

Travis strode down the hallway, and Roger peered into Reginald's office. The professor leaned back in his chair, eyes closed. A steaming cup of tea sat in front of him. Roger wondered if Reginald had fallen asleep until the professor invited him in, without opening his eyes. Roger had a seat, and Reginald opened his eyes to regard his guest.

"Now you've been privy to some of my exciting life! It's a small group, our faculty, and those two have a habit of discussing things with me most evenings during the semester, both fascinating and droll. Have you ever read Creasy?"

Roger shook his head and handed back the folder that the professor had entrusted to him. "I've got everything that I need from that; it was tremendously helpful. I've finished my preliminary drafts—just applying the finishing touches. I don't have any follow-up questions for you regarding the Springs at the moment, but again, thank you."

"I congratulate you," Reginald responded. "I also spoke with Brad Evers today. He won't be harassing you any longer. I informed him that you are a personal friend, and I also assured him that you wouldn't be libeling his business in any way. That should spare you any more trouble, while you're in town."

"Reginald . . . thank you so much!" Roger said, still surprised. "You have made my time here tremendously more pleasant. I think this has cemented the beginning of a strong friendship; I'll always have a good contact in this area for as long as you intend to remain."

"I feel the same way. However, has your curiosity been sated about me now that you have discovered my previous membership in the Astral Yeomen?"

Once again, Roger was impressed and unsettled by the professor's apparent superhuman senses. "Well, it was interesting to discover. I am curious by nature, given my profession. I don't mean to appear a snoop."

"In that case, I'll cover my bases, dispel any notions and misconceptions you may be forming. We would assemble at nighttime, sometimes in a church basement or rotating among different residences of members, and perform various spiritual activities. Occultism. Seances . . . automatic writing sessions, conjuring spirits. One time we all witnessed the appearance of a revenant."

"You mean to say, the visible form of a ghost?" Roger asked, not masking his incredulity.

"I do, and I maintain that's what it was. It did not speak to us but simply danced in place, a silent anomaly that locked my spine in tingling at the sight of it. But you could argue it said a great deal through its forlorn, indescribable expressions before it vanished. Even now, looking back I find that the more likely and simple explanation rather than that all of us mistaking a shape of mist or dust. Do you also know that one time, Sam River and his son both claimed to me that they saw a naked dwarf scurrying in a wood near the Fox River? Wonder surrounds us, but it is veiled," Reginald said, waving his hands outwardly, before catching himself to resume his normal, calm inflection. "My time with the Yeomen was an amusing way to explore the spiritual and sublime aspect of our existence, in an alternate setting to that numbing congregationalism, you could say." He took a swig of his tea, and a brief silence followed. "But it also had diminishing returns, and I excused myself from their number, although I am still friends with and consulted by a good number of them. I am more solitary now, most evenings."

Roger rose from his chair and thanked the professor for his frankness. With a firm handshake, he took his leave and moved briskly to make his date with Lucy. He met up with her outside of the Fountain Spring House. From there they had dinner at the residence of Cynthia Lowell's fiancé, Chad Fenwick. It was a good meal of venison, scalloped potatoes, cooked carrots, and devil's food cake for desert. Unfortunately for Peaches's sake, Roger could find nothing objectionable about Chad. Afterwards, Roger and Lucy bundled up and strolled down to the Red Oak Club, a more formal and comfortable setting for Roger than McGinty's. Over cocktails, the two learned more about each other's pasts and present. Roger began to feel that his bachelor status throughout his twenties had been well worth it with the discovery of Ms. Lucy. Lucy revealed that she had a couple of failed courtships, most of her previous suitors insisted that she cease working at the Spring House to undertake managing the household and rearing children.

"I wasn't ready to say goodbye to the place, or to working, in general. It's too much fun around there anyway, especially in the summer," she said, holding Roger's hand with one and a cranberry juice with the other.

"I don't mind it at all!" Roger replied. "I've never thought much about the prospect of children. I think so long as I had the company of such a wonderful woman, I'd be quite happy in either case!"

Lucy commended Roger that he remained an incorrigible charmer, and that evening allowed Roger to escort her, arm in arm back to her apartment. After stealing kisses with Roger at the doorstep, she spoke. "Despite my reputation as being a non-traditionalist, I will bid you a goodnight here at my doorstep, Roger. Thank you for a lovely evening. You are a gentleman, although you move rather quickly if this is a courtship."

"I'm afraid I don't have much choice in the matter!" Roger replied, his cheeks turning redder than they already were from the cold. "I'm starting to think that I may love you!"

"That's just what I'm talking about!" Lucy said, blushing as well. "And the way you say things like that, so innocently and shamelessly!"

"Well, I should think that it's nothing to be ashamed about!" Roger replied in his defense. After saying goodbye, Roger fell asleep that night looking at the small section of the strange translation and regretted the act in his strange dreams. His last full day in the town dawned as he was greeted by an overcast sky. The morning afforded time for a light breakfast and for Roger to read through his stories, make edits, and insert final additions. He observed he still had the opportunity to stop by the Spring House one last time that evening, meaning perhaps a final meeting with Lucy, at least for this trip. Before the afternoon had fully waned, he seized the chance.

* * *

"Perfectly wonderful, exemplary as always!" a voice called out with a moderate German accent. "He has prepared it upon the rivers; he leads me beside quiet waters," the man finished warmly.

"Thank you, Archbishop. We are delighted with your patronage," Lucy remarked, her eyes spotting Roger as he entered. "Sebastian, here's someone you might like to have a quick chat with."

"Oh? Who's this gentleman?" The bearded man, a silver lion, looked Roger up and down with a deep appraisal.

"Roger Merrick, of the *Chicago Tribune*, at your service," Roger said, a tad off-guard at receiving the firm handshake.

"A Chicago reporter! That is interesting. In Waukesha of all places! You don't mean . . . ah, you are doing a piece on the Spring House?" He paused while Roger nodded. "Well, I can't permit you to be anything but charitable to Ms.

Morris and this immaculate hospitality. Sebastian Gebhard Messmer," he greeted with a pleasant smile. "Not that much charity is needed. The truth should suffice with the excellence of this place!"

"I am in agreement, so no need to worry, your . . . eminence?" Roger grasped at potential honorifics in his head.

"Ah, that is gracious of you, but unnecessary. Out of courtesy everyone has been calling me Archbishop, but I remain humbly the Bishop of Green Bay until my installation this December. Nonetheless, I have enjoyed acquainting myself with the area, and this gem," he gestured with outstretched arms, "has been invaluable in relieving the stress of certain embroiling issues of the Archdiocese. Are you a member of the Church, son?"

"I . . . well, I am Lutheran by upbringing actually, English Evangelical Lutheran Synod of Missouri, and my German is not as good as it should be."

"Well, that is a veritable mouthful," he replied, smiling. "No need to be so uneasy. It seems at first that almost everyone is Lutheran here—there are so many Germans in this part of Wisconsin—and I do get along with them well on account of the language. You may simply call me Sebastian."

"Not a significant change from your native Germany, if I may venture?"

"Close! Switzerland! I did finish my education at Innsbruck, however. I understand it's difficult to place the proper region," he remarked, checking his pocket watch. "Have you seen the dome of our Milwaukee Polish church,

St. Josaphat? The only larger dome in the whole country is in our nation's capital building! You ought to see it before you return to Chicago if time allows. Its magnificence pales compared to the glory of our living God, but I think you'd find it quite a sight, even for a Chicagoan like yourself. It's modeled after St. Peter's in Rome!"

"I shall visit, if not on this trip, then the next time I am by."

"I will caution you, it is not yet complete on the inside, but the stained-glass windows are in. They were also imported from Innsbruck—like me, small wonder! But it would be splendid for you to make a visit. Ms. Morris, Roger, good afternoon." He waved to the valet outside the window, stepping out and casting one last glance back at Roger as he exited.

Roger and Lucy exchanged pleasantries, then walked over to one of the private spaces available at the Springs House. Roger heard a quiet snicker from Cynthia Lowell as they passed out of the lobby. The couple embraced and kissed. "Perhaps we should take a dip?" Roger said nonchalantly, sporting his best sly grin.

"A perfect scandal against the protocols of Springs House employees," Lucy said in mock protest. "But your timing is all wrong, darling. I still have things to attend to before spending a hot hour in a spring, even with someone as handsome as you. But I think your mind is on the right track. Another time perhaps?" Roger returned a wistful look as the two were about to head back into the common hallway. Lucy added, "I suppose if the Springs were to fail, I could pack up and try my luck in Chicago if you think there's room for a woman like me."

Roger wanted to exclaim a thousand celebratory agreements all at once, but managed, "I'd love that." Roger and Lucy parted, and he returned to his hotel. Again, his thoughts rushed ahead to his departure for Chicago tomorrow morning. He finished packing and regarded his collection of article titles: *Waukesha Springs House Primes for Resurgent Holiday Season, Ho-Chunk Powwows: Bridging Communities, and Elusive Haunchyville*, a smirk surfacing at the folly of his final piece. A knock at his door startled him, and he was glad that the repair had finished re-securing his accommodation. "Who's there?" he called without rising from his chair at the desk.

"It's your favorite slugger!" a familiar voice called out. "Buddy, you really need to get out and eat somewhere other than this hotel," the voice continued, muffled through the door. "Do you just hole yourself up like this down in Chicago, too? I've got news for you; it's a pretty big city!"

Roger opened the door and greeted Peaches. The two arranged a final dinner together that evening at a place called Mueller's. Peaches' appearance was still a bruised mess; the swelling had not receded much, and his face was a watercolor of various bruising. The springs water had been soothing on his wounds, but perhaps only exacerbated the swelling. As they walked to the restaurant, Peaches also aired his concerns that he might have tweaked one of his muscles for the long-term, which could get him in serious trouble with his manager.

"It's owned by a farmer named Fred Mueller," Peaches said as the two took their seats. "I found the place by chance, since you've probably noticed it's not too far from the Spring House." Peaches said with a wave of his hand. "Fred actually likes baseball and knew who I was! Turns out he takes his boys for a game, once per season. He's here most nights, but like everywhere else, closes for Sunday. Anyway, I think it's smart for a farmer to branch out, don't you think? You'll definitely notice a bit of a difference from a Chicago steak. At least, I did."

"That's the most I've ever heard you say all at once. I see that talking about food really gets your mouth moving," Roger said, looking at the various steak, potatoes, and vegetable options on the menu.

"Fair enough. So when are you proposing to your gal, then?" Peaches asked, as he looked up from his menu to carefully study Roger's face for the trademark reddening and discomfort.

"You may think that's funny, Peaches, but I may attempt to procure an engagement ring when I get my next advance! In truth, I think it's going to be more difficult securing the time to come back here."

"Woah! You really *are* serious! Good for you, pal. You're not going to sink that poor girl's business to get her to come running to you?"

"Don't be ridiculous. As if she'd overlook such sabotage,

I'd rather not see her wrath," Roger said, while settling on his menu option. "I suppose you have nothing but time in the off-season?"

"No way! I'm actually busier," Peaches laughed. Roger looked up from the menu, surprised. "You think I support myself on only my baseball salary? I wouldn't be eating here if I wasn't installing floors all winter. Granted, people are hesitant about getting a floor refinished or installed during the wintry months. They have concerns over the sludge and what not, but the genius of it is that most of the trades go quiet during the cold. Owners and landlords just need a little convincing, but my buddy Landon, the business owner, he keeps me busy, and fit enough until spring training."

"Again, sounds like your opportunities for romance are limited, unless you are making advances at married women while on the job."

Peaches just laughed at that. "I think you'll need to start a trend of making baseball games a lively dating spot! You and Lucy showing up to some games may do the trick, then some prospects may show up, too, and I'm not talking about baseball players!"

More chitchat followed during a hearty steak dinner. Roger's digestion was only disturbed by the unpleasant sight of Bradley Evers sitting at a table across the room, who offered a glare to Roger before returning to his own meal. Upon settling the bill, Roger was in a state of mild amazement at his nearly empty wallet. As advertised, the owner, Fred, was in attendance that night and visited them at their table.

Roger and Peaches commended him on the quality of the meal and offered casual conversation until Roger mentioned his bizarre interaction and troubles with Thomas Moss.

"Moss?" Fred asked, animated by the name. "He lives in a cottage that he rents on my property, near the edge of a tree line dividing my land from the Seehausens. He works as a bit of a forester, and as a hand during planting and harvest, but I'd be lying if I said I wasn't aware that he finds . . . other employment. I'd like to think he is a decent man, and he often enough is, at least in my presence. I'm sorry, I had no idea he was causing such trouble for you."

"The problem is I don't know the extent of it. He's so damn confusing and mysterious when you actually sit down and talk with him," Roger confessed, then peeked over to make sure Evers wasn't eavesdropping.

"Yeah, now I know for sure that we're talking about the same Tom," Fred said with a slight frown. "I'll say a few words to him next time I see him. From what I can tell, he values his little spot and may need a reminder that it's not a given."

Roger and Peaches left around 7:30 p.m., after a dessert of pie. They were greeted by a cold, slanting rain, and the streets had emptied considerably since they had entered the restaurant. Peaches didn't even propose a night of drinking, confessing that all he wanted was for his body to recover as he pulled his collar to shield his face from the rain. Walking back to the hotel brought them right past the Spring House. A sudden screamed pierced the night through the murmuring precipitation.

"What the good hell?" a frantic Peaches cried. "That sounded like it came from in there!" He pointed straight at the Spring House. "They're supposed to be closed up by now!"

In agreement, Roger led the way without hesitation, his heart racing with concern for Lucy. He ran towards the closest entry door, which appeared to have been forced open. The condition of the handle and scrapes on the door jamb near the lock resembled the method which had been used on his own hotel door. *By God, if Moss had done something . . .* Roger swelled with anger, which overwhelmed his present fear. The interior of the Spring House looked much different without the natural light coming through its generously appointed windows, and none of the electric or gas lanterns were on either. Only the faint glow of one outside street lamp provided some sight within. Roger and Peaches proceeded quietly and as quickly as they could as their eyes adjusted, both having some knowledge of the layout after their visits. Roger had no familiarity with the majority of the larger building, and he wondered if any of the vacant hotel rooms were used as an apartment for the staff during the skeletal months. They began looking into the various changing rooms, which were derelict. That brought them to the paneled sliding door to the one of the interior bathhouses. Roger pressed up to the wall on the left side of the door and thought that he saw the shadow of a silhouette dart by from inside the room, uncertain if it was cast by Peaches, who had crossed behind him to flank the large door from the right-hand side.

They whipped open the door, Peaches stepping in first, who immediately rasped some profanity. Roger stepped in a moment later and discovered a gruesome sight. The slender body of a woman, discernable by the longer hair, was floating on its stomach in the water of the spring, which had been muddled with blood and burnt flesh. Water soaked through and discolored the pouter pigeon shirtwaist and trumpet-skirt, rent with small holes. There was a sizable, arch-shaped breach torn through the wall of the House, facing out to the avenue. Roger ignored this and rushed to the side of the pool, breathing heavily. "Hey! Careful now!" Peaches cried out. Roger tripped and nearly toppled over another body that he hadn't seen on the stone floor of the room in his haste. Even in his state, Roger turned to look at what he had toppled over and instantly recognized the body of Thomas Moss. His bowler hat had been knocked off at some point, revealing long and thinning straw hair underneath. Moss's countenance was unsettling; his eyes were wide and mouth agape in a painful expression.

Roger didn't notice any immediate injury to the man and turned and crouched over the pool. He could feel an intense heat over the waters, more severe than during his regular visit. Tiny bubbles danced upon the surface. *Is it boiling?* Tears or heat and emotion began forming in Roger's eyes as he reached out to the shoulder of the floating body, which was hot to the touch. He put on his gloves, and as gently as possible, pulled the body closer. He slid his other hand underneath the other shoulder as the body drifted closer to the edge, and he gritted his teeth as he felt the pain of the scalding water on his backhand and knuckles, even through the gloves. Grimacing, Roger flipped the body over and had to turn away as he was splashed by the blistering water. He turned his gaze to the face of this victim. It was indeed a young woman, but not Lucy. Roger could recognize the receptionist, Cynthia Lowell. Her skin was dramatically pinkened from the water, and dark spots indicated where blood vessels had burst beneath the skin. Her bun had come undone at some point, causing her auburn hair to cover her shoulders while Roger lifted her out of the water. It was a horrific discovery, and Roger felt guilt in his unspoken relief that the poor soul was not Lucy.

"What a mess," was all that Peaches could muster at first, wiping some moisture from under his eyes. "Good Lord . . . that one there," he pointed at Moss. "That's the guy from the alley and the one you were so interested in— Moss?" Roger nodded in response, silently, still holding up Cynthia Lowell from the sweltering pool. "Wonder what the hell did him in? Scared to death?" Peaches bent down and examined the man briefly, then turned his gaze to the body in Roger's arms. "My God, you don't think something is wrong with the water after all?" Peaches asked, worriedly pawing at his throat. "I suppose she's easier to figure out. For the spring to boil like that? Heat must have done it. But I've never heard of anything like that. We're not above a damned volcano!" Still, Roger sat in silence, leaving his friend to narrate his thoughts. "But what do we do now? Call for the cops? I was hoping it wouldn't be such a long night," Peaches finished with a groan.

"We could leave a sort of, anonymous tip . . ." Roger offered, at last. "It's going to be a difficult crime scene for the investigators. I don't exactly like the notion, and they might be suspicious if they discover we were first on the scene, but there's very little that we could offer in the line of questioning. We don't have anything that they couldn't discover on their own." Roger paused, observing Peaches peeping out of the breach of the building into the misty streets, which were still empty. "I agree that it will be a long road once the authorities arrive. I feel like I could do more good on my own. We'll make things right before all this is over."

"What does that mean?" Peaches asked, planting his back against the interior wall. "Are you going to be playing detective? I wouldn't have guessed you had the heroic streak in you. Buddy, you've got me worried that you are going to do something much stupider than simply going straight to the police."

"I'm not sure yet, and I know that. My mind is pulling me in too many directions right now. I need to think."

"I'll leave it to you in alerting the authorities then. I can't stand this place any longer," Peaches said, with a growing tone of panic. "But don't keep me in the dark, pal! If you're not coming with me now, I guess I'll see you later!" Peaches said, his words trailing back as he scurried down the street, vanishing into the mists.

Roger stooped over Thomas Moss once more, checking

the man's pulse and for anything of a lead. He found a wallet that had a few dollars in it and nothing else, as well as Moss's trusty knife that had been locked in his right hand. Roger left these things behind, his hopes of finding a note or a clue dashed. He was feeling overwhelmed at the opaque scene. He wasn't a detective, but he certainly felt like an investigator as he took a final appraisal. Even after searching Moss more closely, there was no obvious cause of death. The bubbling spring had returned to its normal warmth as Roger exited, suggesting a sudden and bizarre event. His explanations were falling short of anything but the supernatural. *The best way to learn anything is why Cynthia and Moss were both here, after-hours. Cynthia was not moving in with her fiancé until after their wedding date, so could she live in a room on the upper floor? That could explain her presence easy enough. But what was Moss doing here, and how was that breach created? Why was it created? He clearly did some lock-picking to enter. Another person . . . could there have been another person entering with Moss? This person could not have left through the front door; we would have seen them. Then whoever it was exited through this strange rupture in the wall, and probably created it somehow.*

Deciding that he had risked enough time, Roger stepped out through the breach into the broad promenade. The Fountain Spring House had a good deal of space around it, more than most of the tightly packed buildings in the downtown area. *For something to make an opening like that in a stone wall, surely it was tremendously loud. But Peaches and I didn't hear anything walking over from Mueller's. The first thing we heard was Cynthia's scream. So perhaps the gap had been made before then, or somehow, was made silently?* There were no discernible clues out here to indicate where the other person slipped off, so Roger took the path back to his hotel. True to his word, he found a Waukesha deputy on patrol along the way.

"Excuse me sir, I heard a noise . . . from the Spring House," Roger stammered. "Then I heard someone, a woman's voice screaming."

"The Spring House?" The officer replied warily, raising his lantern, its flickering light illuminating suspicion in the lawman's visage. "That's three blocks from here! What makes you say there, and not somewhere else?"

"I was closer to the vicinity then, and I came looking for someone," Roger offered, nervous at his weak explanation. "Please, I think someone may be in danger!"

"All right, please just stay calm sir. I'll head right over. I'm Deputy Knudson. May I quickly have your name as well, please?"

Further deception would go against Roger's instincts. He could not bring himself to lie about his name, especially when he perceived no immediate benefit in doing so. "Roger Merrick. I'm staying at the National Hotel." The response seemed to assuage the officer, who nodded and strode toward the Spring House. Roger had made his peace with his course-of-action up until then, but now had to decide his next move.

Of course, he was fretting terribly about Lucy, wanting to see her. This chain of events would spell doom for the Spring

House, no doubt. But time was of the essence, and Roger trusted that she was safe for the moment, so he returned to his hotel room. It was only nine o'clock, and he could sleep as much as he wanted once he submitted his stories to Lou. He had a drink of spring water and sat down at the writing desk. Roger tasked his mind to unmask the unknown person at the Spring House earlier in the evening. *I know next to nothing of Cynthia Lowell's acquaintances and contacts, apart from Lucy and her fiancé, who weren't there. Thomas Moss could know practically anyone with his mode of business. No, better to say, anyone of ill repute.*

Roger's first theory eventually settled on the double murder being connected to Bradley Evers. Evers wanted the demise of the Spring House as one of his objectives to opening up the waterways of Waukesha for full-scale manufacturing. Moss had worked for him before, and posed a potentially terrible inconvenience; he could testify in being contracted for illegal activity, should Evers's star continue to rise. It seemed that it was not below Evers to rotate the criminal network of the area with the likes of Moss, Jim Smitheran, and that other fellow from the alley that Roger had yet to identify. Any one of those types were excellent candidates for the third person at the Spring House, who Roger believed was responsible for killing Moss after Moss had dealt with Cynthia, or even killing both victims. As for the mysterious manner of deaths, it would be strategic to make it look related to the spring water itself. Roger was no medical expert, Cynthia could have just as easily been drowned, and somehow the water was manipulated, perhaps with added chemicals or some clever reagent to appear deadlier. Moss's death provided the greatest difficulty. He was probably lured under false pretenses by the mysterious other party, or threatened. That should have made for a more violent death or struggle, at least in some noticeable capacity. The theory began to unravel over the details of Moss's demise. Roger would need the assistance of someone with wider connections in town so Peaches would not be of help, and Roger preferred to involve Lucy as little as possible. He would see the professor.

To his good fortune, he was still able to order a coffee down at the bar. Roger was prepared to explain the need to burn the midnight oil, ostensibly for his articles. Apparently, it was not that uncommon, and the bartender Nicholas always kept one pot hot until the bar closed. Roger scribbled a message on a piece of notebook paper that he tore out. He addressed it to Peaches, informing his friend that if he should he come looking for him, he had left to consult Professor Reginald Linden to search for answers. Roger exited the hotel dressed in his heavy jacket, scarf, and gloves. He recollected the location of Linden's house on College Street as he noted his pocket watch, just before ten o'clock. He walked up to the outer gate and opened it gently. Roger braced himself for Linden's response at his late calling, yet nonetheless knocked firmly on the solid oak door, unwilling to risk the trip for the sake of politeness. About two minutes passed from when Roger gave the first of several rounds of knocking when a light shone from within the foyer. Moments later, the door opened and Reginald appeared, with a cane in hand and an annoyed expression.

"Roger . . . what has happened?"

"Two people are dead at the Fountain Spring House."

"Oh my. Well, you'd best come in so you can provide the full account." He had handled the news with a stunning lack of emotion, evoking unmasked astonishment in Roger. "Oh, please don't think me so callous. When I saw you appear at my door at this hour, I surmised the news would be grim. Call it the realist in me, if you like."

The two sat down in the professor's study, and Roger recounted the full tale of the discovery from earlier in the evening. Reginald listened patiently, nodding along with each caveat, but interjected after Roger's description of the bodies. "So there was no obvious cause of death with this Thomas Moss? This is a complicated puzzle indeed, but post-mortem examinations tend to be impeccably thorough these days." When Roger finished and offered his theory, Reginald rose from his chair and crossed over to a coat hanger. He pulled off his slippers in favor of long boots. He also grabbed his cane again. "My legs are in perfect health, but I favor this when traipsing through the countryside. I hope that you're okay to trek in the open country; you look reasonably well-prepared. I think we have quite a night ahead of us, my friend."

"You've already devised a plan?" Roger asked, with suffused relief.

"You've decided on a certain path and did not entrust

110

the matter to the authorities, which I would not advise. But by telling me all of these things, it's obvious that you mean to investigate personally. While the police are not perfect, they do have more resources. You are sure you are resolved to look into this?" Reginald asked, his face expressing a parental scowl.

"I feel that I must. I won't have any peace if I go back knowing I left things unresolved."

"And to think, it is only by chance you heard some disturbance and discovered the ghastly scene at all," Reginald replied, with a regretful tone. "Then I'd say that our path is now clearly laid out. While I do not necessarily encourage this activity, I am amused that you chose to confide in me instead of the police." Roger had neglected to tell Reginald that he had at least directed Deputy Knudson to the scene and now decided to keep that knowledge to himself, construing it as a potential advantage depending on where things went from here. He harbored a grain of superstition for almost everyone in town, and the once irrational words of Jessica Pickett were now starting to gnaw at him in paranoia. "Jack the Ripper undermined public confidence in the police in London," Reginald resumed. "I wonder if the Springs deaths will have a similar effect here? We certainly have become fast friends—or do you have a dark past with the law that you haven't told me about?"

"I can't divulge my trade secrets, Reginald," Roger said slyly, who had expected such glibness from the professor. "So where do you propose we head to first?"

"This Thomas Moss's residence, of course. He seems like the only viable lead from that scene you happened on. Although I don't have the faintest idea where he lives . . . if he indeed has a home at all."

Roger grabbed his folded map of the county out of his case, finding Fred Mueller's land. "Leave that to me."

5

The midnight trip was lent speed and confidence by Reginald's knowledge of the area. The rain had stopped, but the ground was still damp, and only small pockets of starlight cast any illumination in the overcast. Some twenty-five minutes after the two had left, Reginald noted on Roger's map that they were now coming up on Farmer Mueller's land, south of the city. The going was much more strenuous than Roger had anticipated; he had trouble keeping up with the intrepid professor. Roger was surprised that Reginald's knowledge extended far beyond the broad geographic survey in his writings. Reginald never led them astray, always noting to "be careful on this slope," or "keep left to avoid stepping into the marsh." These were the only breaks in the silence of their journey. Roger was too possessed with thought to offer conversation and felt the need to be discreet. At length, Roger spotted a patch of forest that resembled the one mentioned by Fred as the location for the cottage. Sure enough, at the edge of a line of trees bordering thicker woods, a small hovel was nestled. "Is there anything else that you know about this man, Moss, before we go further? You don't suppose anyone else may happen on this place while we investigate?"

"I can't make any such guarantees," Roger replied truthfully. "If word spreads that something's happened to him, I would say it's likely he may have some visitors asking after him if he fails to make an appointment, or even to quickly ransack the place, if there's anything of value. You've been a great help, professor. I'd understand if you wish to recuse yourself from this point and not venture further. I'd wager I could make my way back to town from here, even if it takes me twice as long as it did for you in guiding us here."

"Now Roger, I've come with you this far. I may be the difference between you making it out of this night alive, incarcerated, or otherwise. I'm quite too invested to withdraw now," he finished, reassuringly.

There was a low wooden fence with a convenient gap that the pair moved through. Unsurprisingly, there was no smoke coming out of the chimney. The ragged roof looked about five years past replacement, and the wooden door showed early signs of rot, but it was shut securely. Reginald immediately pushed on it, though it did not yield.

"I don't presume you despoiled him of any kind of key when you found him?" he asked, looking back to Roger.

"I didn't find one, but I certainly didn't dare at the time to be thorough. Let me have a look." Roger studied the door, finding no clues in its design. "Perhaps we should swing around once?" The two did just that, finding that the cottage had two windows—one on the south side, near the door, and another on the western face. The north side of the home, which faced directly toward the woods, had a lonely shed with a loose-hinged door that opened. Inside there were some rusted tools that swayed gently, emitting a forlorn creaking, although Roger could discern no breeze. Amidst the squalor, a single key hung from a small hook that was partially concealed under an ingrown vine. Roger grabbed the key and returned to the door. He tried the key and with a squeak, opened the lock granting entry to the cottage.

"Well done, Roger. It's a shame that the nature of this evening's activities likely will render them unfit for your articles."

"Perhaps the path to my Pulitzer begins in this cottage," Roger replied, trying to mask his unease.

Moss's home was a filthy heap of a cabin. Despite the vacancy of its occupant, Roger could feel Moss's presence represented in the very untidiness of the space. The main room of his home was ill-lit, a single candle had burned low on a table that had a couple of notebooks and a plate of spoiling meat. The earthen floor felt sloped in this crowded space. Two additional rooms could be seen off to the left and right from their perspective: an unmade bed in one and a small kitchen in the other. Of most immediate interest were the notebooks, and Roger gingerly picked up the top one, hearing Reginald close the front door, and began leafing through the pages.

"This top one appears to be his way of managing his finances. Just a list of purchases . . . have a look if you like." Roger casually tossed it back onto the table, regretting the action as the motion of the flying notebook nearly snuffed out the candle.

Reginald did not venture in as deeply as Roger and instead kept an eye outside, systematically peeking his head to check for anyone coming. " I'm surprised he's literate at all, from how you described him," Reginald replied, without removing his view from the window. "Nothing suspicious? I would have guessed some chemicals could achieve that effect you witnessed at the Springs House, but it's quite possible he wouldn't even make a log of any of his more incriminating acquisitions."

Roger nodded silently in agreement, placing the notebook down and examining the one underneath. Upon turning to the first page, Roger noticed at the top the date of January 1, 1902. A brief account of that day and the preceding Christmastide followed in untidy script. It appeared that he had found Moss's personal diary. The entries were not logged daily, and at times more than a month seemed to elapse from the last page. Moss had taken some pride in creating some moonshine toward the end of last year and mourned the loss of a dog named Jasper. He noted his results of a few card games, where he typically lost, and only reported the amount he gained from rare wins. Moss had a good opinion of his landlord, Fred Mueller, who deferred rent payment or substituted it for various labor on his farm. Most of the entries consisted of completed jobs or contracts that Moss had taken on for Fred Mueller in this capacity or the various sorts of other opportunities in the area. Clearing weeds and thickets, collecting debts, roughing people up, pilfering a store or a residence—there was a full litany of menial or criminal activities documented. Roger leafed through very quickly to place himself at about a month's time ago, in mid-September, 1903. From here, Roger began the more wearisome task of reading Moss's mundane reports more carefully in the dim and unfriendly space. At no time had Moss mentioned the Spring House, or Cynthia, or Lucy. "You seemed to have found something interesting to keep your nose between those pages for so long," Reginald commented, and indeed Roger was unsure of how long he had been reading.

"It's Moss's diary, such as it is. I'll confess it's intrigued me. I'll let you know when I make it to recent events." Reginald nodded and impatiently checked his watch. Roger resumed his reading and gave his full attention to the final set of entries, the first dated October 1, 1903:

E.S. and I set out for Haunchyville today. Promised payment of forty dollars for guiding him successfully. Came to the spot in the early evening after I led him around by the nose for a good part of the day. I wanted to see some haunchers, and saw more than ever! Something had them all riled up. Left the place, but E.S. didn't make it. No money from this job. Probably never be seeing him again. Never seen a reaction like that out of the buggers either, must not have liked his smell. Too bad, I warned him that they cut men down! I told him not to go wandering around in Haunchyville! Wonder if they gnawed him down to size? Maybe he's dancing around with them now? Don't know who to tell about E.S., if anyone. Didn't seem like a family man.

October 17, 1903: Haven't seen E.S., he's definitely done

for. Mr. Mueller says I need to pay cash this month. Found a job for B.E., roughing up some out-of-towner. R.M. had a buddy who could hit like an ox. Guy threw a baseball and broke J.S.'s nose! Rotten luck for us, B.E. only gave me ten dollars. Going to need more work before month's end. Tomorrow: check for work with R.L., sell story to R.M.?

October 20, 1903: Big job for R.L. tonight, a little "door maintenance" and footwork. Might move out of here tomorrow. I ought to leave some cash still for Mr. Mueller, best man around here. I hear land is cheap around Eau Claire right now. Don't mind being further away from Haunchyville either.

Roger's heart was racing. The connections were laid bare for him in Moss's diary. E.S. was undoubtedly the hoaxer Eugene Shepard, who had gone missing some time ago. Roger had resisted suspecting Reginald Linden, as he been a good friend and useful contact. But now the professor was implicated in Moss's diary—barring the chance that Moss's initial system was referring to someone else. Linden and Moss both had a connection to Shepard, who had marshalled information from Linden and assistance from Moss in his ill-fated quest to find Haunchyville. Moss and Linden must have established a line of contact from that interaction, or even had associations before Shepard's arrival, yet Reginald continued to play off that he had no former contact with him. *What had Reginald wanted with Moss recently? To break into some places for him? Like my room at the hotel or the Springs House? To murder someone? Was Reginald the third person at the Spring House?*

Roger turned at a faint sound of clutter being disturbed to see that Reginald had crept very near with his signature stealth, as when Roger had first examined the loaned folder in the professor's study. His silent approach failed him only at the last moment due to the claustrophobic untidiness of the space. Roger closed the diary as nonchalantly as he could manage, while still clutching it guardingly. "You had gone quiet again," Reginald said, forming a rare smile. "You must have seen something compelling in the journal! Come now, don't hog it all for yourself!"

"He really seemed to believe in that Haunchyville. Apart from that, nothing too extraordinary, and no entries starting from almost a month ago." Roger swallowed, his throat going dry.

Reginald was silent for a moment, and Roger sensed doubt in the professor's countenance. "Ah, well if that's the case, it seems that my idea wasn't so good after all. I thought we'd turn up answers. Sorry to drag you out here." If Reginald was now feigning disinterest in the diary, it was magnificently performed. "Perhaps we must indeed entrust this case to the authorities and return to town? You're leaving tomorrow, as I recall?"

"That sounds good," Roger said weakly, and he reminded himself to breathe. *If Reginald had reason to harm me as well, this would be the perfect place to do it. Another "victim" of Moss for the police to find after the Spring House.* Roger tentatively moved toward the door of the cottage, where Reginald still stood watching Roger approach.

"Be that as it may, "Reginald began, arms folded as he leaned against the only exit, "I would like a quick view at that diary for our trouble venturing out here. I suppose you intend to take it with you since you're still holding it?" He stretched out his hand, and Roger hesitated. "Well come now! What is this? There's something in there that you don't want me to see perhaps? We're friends, aren't we Roger?" he asked earnestly.

"I don't know!' Roger blurted out. "You need to come clean about your connection with this Moss fellow! It is now apparent that there are things you aren't telling me, which I would not press you about, but there you have also misled me on some matters since our first interactions. What is your game here? Go ahead, find your name in the damned diary!" Roger threw the diary to him, unable to think of anything else.

"Roger . . . Roger! There's no need to get so upset over a misunderstanding. My connections with Moss, he's . . ." but at that point, Reginald abruptly stopped and pivoted away from the door, crouching against the interior wall. "Someone is out there!"

Sure enough, discernible through the muddy window, there were three distinct figures approaching the cottage with some haste from the fields opposite the woods. Reginald seemed genuinely surprised at the arrival of the newcomers, and Roger momentarily put aside his suspicion. Only one of them carried a lantern, but even that face was obscured by the outer darkness and grime of the window panel. A growing murmuring suggested that they were having a discussion while they approached.

"It's no use hiding in here!" Reginald hissed, and stood to his full height with his hand on the door. "If they enter they'll certainly discover us! I can't imagine they're the nicest of fellows, but I think I will announce our presence to them. I'd rather deal with explanations than itchy trigger-fingers if they're armed!"

"For all I know they're with you!" Roger countered at the convenient timing of the new arrivals.

"This is simply childish. After we deal with this situation, I assure you, I will explain everything to you, but we don't have time with brigands at the door!"

Roger thought to offer a counter-strategy but could find nothing better at that moment. At the very least he was convinced at the professor's surprise at the arriving men. He gave Reginald a nod and instead began to feel a swell of relief that whoever had arrived may have saved him from the designs of the great enigma of Reginald Linden. He would do his best to take advantage of the situation.

"Oi there!" Reginald called out. "Don't be alarmed. We're inside of the cottage. It's Reginald Linden and Roger Merrick. I'm going to open the door now." Roger hoped that Reginald's voice, which was very loud and clear inside, was not too muffled by the stuffy cottage to reach the ears of those outside. Reginald opened the door and stepped through the threshold, and he beckoned Roger to do the same. Roger went out and could see the flanking men much better. He recognized two of them at once: Jim Smitherman and the man with the ox-faced from the alley. The third face was new, a man with pale skin, clean shaven, and greasy black hair like a mop on his head. But Roger had a good idea of the type of person that would consort with these two. They seemed to have a penchant for working in threes. Jim Smitheran and the new fellow each wielded a shotgun, and the ox-faced man carried the lantern.

"Well now, the good professor had some business with our old friend Moss again," Jim Smitheran said through some tobacco in his mouth, sounding stuffy with his broken, taped nose from three nights ago. "Though this is a surprise, you making a house call. A bit beneath your station, isn't it Professor?" When he got no response, he asked another question. "Moss in there?"

"No, he is not," Reginald answered. "Moss is dead, and I don't have the faintest idea what you're going on about."

That certainly surprised Smitheran, who spit out an impressive wad of tobacco at the news. "Dead? First I've heard of it! Did you two kill him where he slept? Your reporter friend covering the big story? I still owe him a beating!" He waved his gun at Roger and let out a drawling laugh when Roger flinched in turn. "Too bad about Moss. We are here on account of some debts of his. How did he go, if you don't mind?"

"We don't know that, and we'll be leaving now," Reginald responded. "We'll neglect to mention to the authorities that we saw you here. I'll be so bold to trust that you'll have the sense to return the courtesy, not that you would ever say a word to them, outside of a holding cell!" Reginald had spoken briskly and began pacing forward for a gap between them.

"I agree, our meeting here is best kept private, but not before we'll relieve you both of your cash, and then leave a little something to remember us by," Smitheran said, moving to block them as they tightened in to close off the area near the gap in the fence. "No big ball player to save you this time, city-slick," he said more softly, now that he had drawn closer to Roger.

Roger didn't mind so much handing over what meager money remained in his wallet but bristled at the prospect of a thrashing. There was simply nothing he could do against the armed men. Smitheran first approached Reginald, warily lowering his gun slightly as he outstretched his other hand to relieve the professor of his wallet. Reginald cast a glance back to Roger, then gestured with a sideways nod to the other brigand with the shotgun. *What, he wants me to deal with him somehow?* The idea was impossible, but then Reginald reached for his pocket in apparent submission. Instead, he suddenly lunged out and grabbed Smitheran's forearm with both of his hands. Reginald then bellowed out in a confounding, harsh tongue as Smitheran twisted in surprise and raised his gun.

A visible tremble of heated air and pressure shot out from Reginald's hands. The wave of energy unfurled in a wide cone shape from the professor's grip towards Smitheran and the other assailants at his flanks. It must have been very hot, as Roger could feel an explosion of heat, even from where he was standing opposite of the blast. The effect was strangely silent; all that emitted was a low and crackling groan. Blood splattered all the way onto the tops of Roger's shoes, and he saw that the droplets boiled as they sizzled their indentations into the leather surface. Fighting paralysis of fear and confusion, his desire to avoid being shot drove his wobbling legs toward the stunned, greasy-haired man with the shotgun, who had dropped the weapon and fallen to his knees. The man had covered his face with his hands, the backs of which showed mild burns and a type of shriveling from that flash of heat.

Roger grabbed the shotgun, confirmed that it was loaded, and seized a few extra shells that had spilled out of the man's pockets onto the ground. It was a double-barreled model with two triggers, the same type that his uncle George had used on hunting trips. Roger was unsure where he should aim the gun. Smitheran appeared to be nothing more than a pile of scorched clothes near the blasted earth where he had stood. Reginald was contending with the ox-faced man, who seemingly recovered swiftly from the magical assault and had the fortitude to hold his ground. He had laid hold of Reginald's arms, and was grappling him to the ground. Hearing movement just beneath him, Roger turned the shotgun and clubbed the greasy-haired man hard in the face with the butt of the weapon. The man's head thudded back into the turf, and Roger raised the shotgun towards the ox-faced man struggling with Reginald. He didn't have a clear shot for either one in particular, and so approached closer. "It's over! That's enough! I've got your buddy's gun!"

"Don't shoot me, shoot him!" the ox-faced man exhorted. This was the first time Roger had heard the deep voice, and it was clearly terrified. There was a look of dread on his face as he still clutched on to Reginald. "Didn't you see what he did to the others? You've been walking around with the Devil!"

"For God's sake Roger, help me!" Reginald shouted. "You have nothing to fear from me!"

Thinking instinctively, Roger aimed in the middle of the tangled legs of his targets. He was now at close range, and slightly favored the barrel of the gun toward the ox-faced man. He fired. Immediately both men dropped and cried out in pain. Roger had intended to do more harm to the ox-faced man, and indeed, Reginald grabbed his cane and sprung toward the recovering brute. The cane opened, producing a sword that extended from the handle which was now detached from the rest of the shaft. There was a struggle, but the weapon gave Reginald an edge against the recovering man. He sawed the blade at the man's neck, whose hands were bleeding from holding back the attack. A few moments later, he succumbed as his throat was cut open, a messy end for the man who jerked in pain, rasped, and went still. Roger instinctively backed away several paces from the professor, hoping that he was not in the range or intent of the man's deadly magic or swordplay.

"That was bloody stupid of you!" Reginald snarled, struggling to stand while covered with the man's blood. He had too hastily re-affixed his cane, and as it bore his full weight, the handle buckled, and the professor toppled over as the neck of the cane snapped. Roger saw that Reginald's right trouser leg was shredded in numerous places, and blood was beginning to drip down.

"Reginald, what the hell is that . . . *craft* that you used?" Roger cried out, shakily leveling the gun at the professor. "Good Lord, what's a man supposed to think when he sees nightmarish powers like that? Now I believe I can piece out what happened at the Spring House tonight, after what I've seen what you're capable of! Self-defense and even Moss are one matter, but why the hell that poor woman Cynthia Lowell? What's the point of all of this?"

"Moss and the woman? Their deaths will assuredly lead to the closing of the Spring House, as you must have already perceived. It draws too many tourists to the area, where secrets must be kept, for now. Its continuing existence is ill-suited to my interests, and it allowed for the removal of Moss as well. I thought you'd be able to write a balanced article to finish the long decline of that bloated resort. You should have just went back to Chicago, but when I saw how insistent you were on playing investigator, it became necessary to see what you would uncover this night. Be grateful I showed you mercy in sparing that manager you're infatuated with!"

Roger bristled at that, which elicited a rare and brief smile from the professor, starkly white along with his eyes, compared to his bloodied face. "If you are really concerned about nature, why go after people like that?" Roger started, his thoughts turning again to Lucy's safety. "When you know that there are people like Brad Evers, who wouldn't give a second thought to all of the springs being devoured in his enterprise? You're talking madness, but it's not even consistent with itself!"

"If you must know, I'm afraid that Evers Automation is no threat at all. His business will collapse within a couple of years. He doesn't have a sustainable business model to compete with the larger outfits—I've studied it, and it will be absorbed," Reginald replied vacantly. "You disappoint me. You are not grasping the higher truths of your situation. You don't think that I have not considered all things with the utmost detail? I have . . . obtained knowledge," he said with new audacity, collecting himself. "I see things differently now. I see everything differently! I grasp what is truly important." His eyes smoldered with a vengeful intensity, never flickering away from Roger's. "What is of value . . . the lost tribe worshipped it. They drew power from it, as I do now." He placed his left hand firmly on the ground and was able to rise to one knee. "Modern society infringes on consecrated arcana, the pearl of my sanctuary. I'm beset by all fronts. Industry, tourism, the inexorable spread of agriculture to feed a burgeoning nation. When your eyes are opened to the whole cosmic truth of things, the meaninglessness of our own societies and lifespans remove your former blindness. It brings focus. It brings fervent peace. I have sought allies in this struggle, who only slowly can be brought into the full reality so that it does not addle their delicate minds. I had hoped you could be one such ally, but you proved too curious for your own benefit. Too greedily you chased after things you had no understanding of. You could not be privy to the subtle path of wisdom. To know what I know, in your state, you would seek to claw out your eyes, and bleach your mind." With this proclamation, he willed himself to his feet, standing tall and grim.

"So I'm to die too, then?" Roger shouted, defiantly. "You've pledged yourself to worshipping some forgotten god and forsake your fellow man? Anyone could be on the verge of becoming just one more obstacle?" Roger's voice quavered, but he was steadying his sight on the chest of the looming magician before him. "You're insane, and I'm putting you down before you can hurt anyone else!"

As Roger pulled the trigger, the ox-faced man's body levitated and lurched unnaturally in front of Reginald, like a marionette tugged from the hand of an unseen giant across the prairie. It served to partially block the shot, but Roger saw both bodies once again hit the ground, and he ran in the opposite direction—for the woods. *I'm not even sure I could kill him. He's like a demon summoned from the Book of Revelation. God, Lord Jesus, please help me!*

After his silent prayer, Roger's adrenaline sent him sprinting past tree and bramble. He had a limited concept of direction but knew that Fred Mueller's plot was south of the Fox River. If he could find the Fox, he could simply follow it upstream until he made it back to the city. He chose the woods to break line-of-sight with any pursuers. Roger saw a strange coloration in the sky above, a gradient from a deep red to a golden color. He remembered the sight from the night of the powwow. After what he had witnessed with Reginald, he could not let a bizarre sky dismay him. He kept moving. The trees grew denser here and Roger winced at the tremendous amount of racket he made as each footfall disturbed dead leaves. The roots on the ground also had an odd characteristic to them. They seemed to wander upwards and grew out in a strange pattern, ominously forsaking the soil from which they came. At last Roger came to a mighty oak. Out of breath and exhausted, he sat down with his back to the generous trunk. The air was cold, and Roger could see his breath, yet he wiped the sweat from his brow and savored the taste of the brisk air as he recovered.

Not a minute after he began his rest, he heard a very faint movement among the detritus in the distance—from the same direction that he had just came. As the sound grew closer, it became apparent that someone was pursuing him. Roger peeked from around the tree to see Reginald Linden, perhaps fifty yards away.

"You chose a very poor direction to flee Roger. I can sense your presence!" he said with a raised voice, steadily advancing. "Uncanny, how straight your path was. You have walked right into the den of all that remains of the lost tribe. Pathetic creatures . . . much like an uncontacted people, but something clearly transformed them . . . or theirs could have been a servitor race." His mumbling ceased as he became aware of his digression. "Destiny has led you here Roger, and you will not escape me, here of all places. You may face your final moment with some dignity, or I will chase you down as prey. It makes no difference!"

Roger bolted from his spot, heading further away from Reginald and into the deepest part of the woods. He could hear Reginald laughing as he ran, and he happened on yet another strange sight. He had come into a type of clearing. Here there was a circle of trees that leaned inwardly, like the town center of a miniature people. They all appeared long dead, bearing no leaves, as if some greater organism below had long consumed their lifeforce. In the very middle of the circle there was a low and smoothly cut stump, like some sort of grand feasting table or altar. The whole place had an otherworldly and abhorrent feel to it. Roger could not continue running and reloaded both barrels of the shotgun with the extra shells he had grabbed. His final shots were ready. A shadow crossed his mind. *I could end my own life to protect my friends. Lucy, Sam, Peaches—he need not come after them if what I know dies with me. But if I'm gone, and he does decide to stretch out his hand against them . . . then all I have done is withdrawn myself from their defense. An atrocious gamble. A coward's gamble. I know that I could never live with that, and I certainly won't die like that!*

Roger aimed the shotgun back toward his pursuer, knowing the shot would be inaccurate at this range, so he waited. Reginald responded tauntingly, outstretching his arms and turning his palms upward like an ancient celebrant. Roger's fingers began tightening on the triggers as he prepared to meet his end, one way or another. But then, a hissing sound called out to him from one of the trees. Roger scanned the circle to identify where the sound had originated, and he spotted a small opening in the base of one of the tree trunks. As he peered deep into that darkness, wondering and doubting at what he heard, again, the hissing called out to him. Roger turned to see that he had lost sight of Reginald, who may have been flanking him at that moment from cover. With that, Roger crouched down to enter, but found that he was still too tall for his head to clear into the tunnel. With no light and only the calling voice to guide him, he again appealed to heaven before trusting to subterranean salvation.

6

The air was stale and close, but it was not as dark as Roger had anticipated. As he descended through the tunnel, the fading light from the dim canopy of the forest was replaced by a strange yellow aura. The source of this light was from the luminescent and thin veins of roots from within the tunnel that weaved together in a tremendous patchwork lining the walls. Roger expected to see some half-man leap out at him at any moment. Indeed, suddenly his crawling hand felt flesh, and with a start, he swung with the butt of the shotgun at the huddled shape. He then realized he had found the corpse of a naked dwarf of a person. But upon inspecting it, the face did not look entirely human. Even in the weak light, it was defined by a great protruding jaw and hooded, black eyes. He thought he could hear a distant voice calling out from above, and if this route had frustrated the professor's pursuit, Roger would not let this discovery deter him. He turned a bend in the tunnel, his eyes now adjusting so that he could see a little distance ahead. He continued to crawl and at last see something, or someone. There was another bent figure ahead, tucked away in a dark offshoot from the main tunnel which continued to descend. The corpse in the cavity seemed human-sized. Roger approached to examine the body, when wide and bright eyes popped open, locking on to Roger's. They were tremendous blue vessels, but had a certain lifelessness to them, as if the spirit inside had already departed.

"You heard my voice." The man, the resuscitated corpse, formed an efforted smile. His teeth were a deeply stained hue, matching the color of the hanging veins surrounding him. "I could tell you weren't a little one. You can feel the vibrations of full-sized feet down here." His hand brushed against the earthen ceiling. "I wanted to help one of my own kind, before the end. You must be a sort of wretch to have come down here."

"I . . . yes, I do need help," Roger stammered, still struggling with what he was witnessing. The man had a full beard, although he seemed to be rapidly losing his hair. He had uneven bald patches on his head and even gaps in his beard. Near him was the body of another of the "little ones." His legs also appeared extremely injured; only remnants of his trousers remained below the knee. The exposed flesh of his lower legs was rent with claw and teeth marks, and dried blood caked the floor that they rested on. Sundered skin and burst blood vessels presented a gruesomely bruised and swollen appearance. The worst was yet to come. His feet displayed split bones and dislocated toes jutting out in different directions, and whole chunks of skin were completely gone, exposing infected sores and bone beneath. *If he could use his legs, indeed if he could even still feel them, the pain must be unbearable. It's a small miracle he hasn't died from the amount of blood he has lost. Was that a failed amputation? What did this to him?* "I would like to help you, as well," Roger mustered at last.

"Help me?" He wheezed a weak laugh. "There's not much that can be done for me now. I will die here and return to the earth, it seems. You can't keep your eyes off of my poor legs. No, of course you can't. The little ones did that to me. I thought I would have died many days ago. I killed some as they gnashed and clawed at me. I was smart. They could only come one at a time for me, here." Again, he brushed his hand against the low ceiling and demonstrated there was only a little space behind him: a defensible alcove. "But with each day I spent trapped down here, the less they paid heed to me, scurrying by with a glare, or avoiding me altogether with a kind of . . . familiarity."

"How long have you been down here? How did you not die of thirst or hunger?"

"You're surrounded by nourishment, newcomer! It's the roots!" He reached with exertion beyond the great bare patch of roots he had made in the vicinity closest to him and cut one out of the wall with a pocketknife. "My own food supply ran out over a week ago." He glanced over to an empty backpack on the tunnel's floor. "The roots have water and some nutrition. Very strong taste, like ginseng! I'm sure the little ones eat this all the time! I'm probably becoming more like them. I also collect a little water when a good rain trickles down," he finished, chewing and swallowing the root with some difficulty. The man's stench hit Roger, and he gagged. "I can only soil the ground around me, I'm afraid," he replied, knowingly. "I'm in no state to move one inch. But maybe I can help you, before my time is over here. My name is Eugene."

"Eugene? Eugene Shepard! You created the Hodag myth! People know that you're missing!"

"Created? No! I did not create it! The Hodag came before me. I just gave the people one to gawk at . . . I gave substance to the story. It's always extraordinary, the power it has on people, many who are holding out for a handful of myths, just waiting to believe anything that lends it a shred of truth. I think we are like that, by nature, searching for hints of fantasy in our lives! And now I'm known as a hoaxer, and no one has cared to look for me, and no one will miss me when I'm gone, either." At this he coughed, a great, deep-seated cough that brought up blood and perhaps a speck of bile. "What's your name?"

"Roger. I'm a reporter, a journalist out of Chicago."

That brought new energy to Eugene. "Well now! Maybe you can tell my story then. Let people know that there are things out there. Creatures . . . energies . . . powers . . . powers," he said wispily, and Roger thought he died on the spot. His head gave a shake, and his eyes returned to focus. "Let me help you now, Roger," he whispered.

"There's a man nearby who wants to kill me," Roger explained. "He too knows of these . . . powers. He also seems to be familiar with this place. Do you know where else this tunnel leads? Is it connected to the others? I suppose I just need to get out of here."

"The tunnels. I've never taken this one all the way. I've mainly been in this spot since I took refuge. The little ones seem to avoid going down there, or maybe they take another way down now that I'm here. You can always go back the way you came." Roger just shook his head at this in response. "Oh, right, you're on the run. I can't promise you anything about what you may find below, but I can still help you." He reached into his jacket pocket with great care and produced a curved dagger. He gave the weapon an admiring glance then extended a trembling hand out toward Roger. "It's yours now."

The dagger had a hilt of bone from an unknown creature, but the material of the curved blade itself was difficult to determine. It had a crystalline complexion tinged with that same yellow hue that prevailed throughout this place. It was razor sharp to the touch. A hollowed space had been made in the pommel which was inlaid with a substance of amber. "It seems like quite the weapon. It looks ancient! Where did you find this?"

"Down here, not far from where you find me now. It was hanging amidst some of the roots in the tunnel, like the fruit of whatever species this is. Maybe a clever hiding spot for its original wielder? Perhaps it's been grown from this very earth! Once I grabbed it, I haven't since encountered any of the little ones."

"Thank you, friend," Roger replied, his eyes welling with

tears. "I'm sorry for what's befallen you. I wish I could do more to help you."

"My own path led me here—and a rat of a man named Tom Moss." Each word that was spoken now was more hoarse and rendered with effort. "I've learned to make my peace with that fact and what time I have left. I think that I shall rest soon. But I would like to get a piece of that man, even still." He coughed for nearly half a minute after saying this and keeled over on his side.

"Don't worry about Moss anymore. He's dead," Roger said, relieved he could bring some bit of news to the tortured soul.

"Is that so? I didn't expect I should outlive him." A crooked smile came to his lips. "Just maybe you can write about me. Something full of . . . honesty. Not like how I've lived." At this he closed his eyes, and no longer regarded Roger.

Roger carefully placed the dagger in his belt loop and marveled at the providence of his timing in finding Eugene in his moments before death. He continued carrying the shotgun that he had recovered although it made the going slower and more difficult in this space. *Having one final shot could make all the difference if I encounter Linden again, or, one of those "little ones."* Parting from Eugene, Roger descended deeper down the tunnels. On a whim, he sampled one of the hanging roots as his stomach growled. It did have an acidic and bitter taste, but quickly Roger noted that he felt energized and could actually see a little bit better in this dimness. He finished consuming the whole segment he had broken off and continued moving, driven by the purposes of survival and the dread of being trapped here like Eugene. Facing Reginald Linden again would take all of his courage, but Roger found it increasingly preferable to the grim decay and regret that colored his recent interaction. Ahead in the tunnel, Roger could see branching paths—the left moved upward and appeared even more narrow than the one he had been traversing, and the right path continued downward. He paused, unsure which direction to take. He prayed for a sign, remembering biblical figures who had done the same. He then worried at this, also vaguely remembering reprimands in some of the accounts for doing so, being of little faith.

At that moment, a scuttling creature appeared, skittering up from the right path. Roger's eyesight was still fuzzy as he strained to focus on the small figure. Had it not been for Eugene's accounts of the haunchymen and already having encountered a dead one, it would have given Roger one hell of a start. It was still all that he could do to keep from panicking, and he silently checked his compulsion to gasp or move. In turn, the creature also halted, swiveling its oversized head to regard Roger. It hunched down, planting its fists on the ground defensively. It had an air of curiosity about its expression and in the twisting of its head, which did nothing to endear its detestable visage. A type of rumbling came from below; loose dirt and rubbish plumed all around. This was enough to break the stalemate and startle the creature away, who chose the left passage, moving with surprising quickness. Roger had received satisfactory indication for his path; he had no intention of taking the same way as the creature. He laughed, grimly, resolved to go into the belly of the beast.

Upon taking this way, Roger rapidly discovered that the descent of tunnel's slope was leveling out, and was becoming airier, with increased headroom. Eventually, he no longer had to crawl and could move forward on his own two feet. Moving hunched over in this way was not much faster, but Roger felt considerably better in moving more naturally. The hanging silence of the tunnel suddenly lifted, as Roger could now hear a faint sound. *Moving water? An underground river? Is that what shaped these tunnels?* Encouraged by the rushing water, he moved with renewed strength, and to his great relief could at last stand again at full height. His back already ached with early soreness that would only worsen. Moments later, he came into something of a cavern as the walls and ceiling of the cave opened around him.

He was in a large grotto. At the center was a spring, which reflected the luster of the luminescent roots. This provided just enough illumination to begin making out the other features of the cave. The increased moisture of the room also supported various lichen and mold species, some varieties shared in the glittering display of light that was reflected in the pool of the spring. From the pool, a stream issued forth that led out of the cave on the opposite side from where Roger entered. Another feature was some rock deposits on the wall, flanking where Roger had entered. Displayed on the sheer surface of the rock wall was the chalk drawing of a spiral. The spiral had labels at various points along its path, which would often fragment and create additional layers to the overall shape. The labels were written with the same mysterious characters that Roger observed in the tome in Reginald's study. It struck Roger that it may be some sort of map, but he could not discern the scale or intent of the bizarre cave-drawing. On the ground near Roger there were some heaped bone fragments, small mammals, and maybe some humans as he saw a skull, silently regarding him.

Finally, on a cramped mound of dirt that rose out of the spring, there was a strange tree. Its coiling roots gripped and writhed around the small island, and its odd and misshapen branches unfurled upward in countless, weaving directions. Hanging from its twisted arms were odd polyps instead of leaves, resonating with some insidious glow. Yellow droplets occasionally fell from the pods, which themselves looked overripe and at the point of bursting, and they stained the earthen mound with sallow spots. Merely looking at the unnatural tree inspired loathing and nausea; the air felt less close, but more fetid, and soon Roger felt a certain light-headedness coming on.

The trunk and lowest branches of the tree did not have the same yellow radiance, but were a midnight black, darker than the rock walls of the cave. "Welcome to a hidden tributary of the Fox, not even noted in my *Geography*," a familiar voice called. Reginald Linden stepped from behind the trunk of the tree. He had discarded his coat, and his forest green collared shirt had been shredded in numerous areas from the shotgun blast, revealing a fit and pale physique in the tattered and bloody openings. Reginald's face, illuminated by the shifting light of the water's surface, showed no discomfort in the damp, cool air despite his frayed outfit. "The stream runs for about a quarter mile that way," he said in a didactic tone, "flowing all the way underground until it joins up with the river. This small cavern was the sacred place of at least one set, perhaps many unnameable peoples. But at least one group amongst them attained a great culture, mapping the stars and channeling the dark energies that only await our access. I must commend you, it was spirited of you to come here by way of the tunnels! Did you see the little ones?"

"Your . . . sanctuary," Roger replied wearily. "So your masked consortium of unsavory contacts, murder, dark magic—it's all to protect this gangly tree and a few cave drawings? Won't the haunchy people take care of that for you?"

Reginald seemed stimulated by that proposition, leaning against the tree. "No, they won't. They are quite unfit stewards! Their population is dwindling, they have been sterile for some time. I've only surveilled the little troglodytes for a few years, but that told me enough. They'll be gone within a generation or two—human generations, I mean. All that will remain of Haunchyville," this last word being pronounced with elevated disdain, "will be a collection of odd tree husks in an otherwise ordinary wood, touched by the distortion of legend and memory. As for this 'gangly tree,' anyone who isn't a barbarian could see it for what it is—a beautiful sight in its uniqueness. Verily, this appendange, like many others, is connected to the heart of the Rooted Whisperer, who dwells further below, where no one can reach him. Still in a delicate state, but slowly, gaining nourishment, soon invulnerable." A thick and large droplet had formed from one of the yellow polyps from the branches which fell into the cupped hands of the professor, who then brought it to his lips. "Perhaps you need only to take a closer look, Roger," he finished snidely, waiting for a response.

"I think I'm fine right here, thank you. Do you think announcing strange names and imagined visions gives you justification for your actions? It seems like you can vaporize people, levitate bodies around like toys, do things that charlatans only stage, or that the delusional dream of, but your greatest feat is still dancing around the point!" Roger said, finding courage through spouting mockery. "You dig out tangents and say nothing of meaning with a whole score of words!"

"If I were truly mad, would you expect me to explain it to you, as you've so clumsily posited?" Reginald intoned, quietly. "I know that you're in journalism, but don't you realize that some things are better shown than told? You want to know the source of my power, why I go to such great lengths? That is something that I can grant to you, an ill-deserved boon, although you do not know what you ask. Receive my final gift before you go to your oblivion."

Reginald placed both of his hands upon the tree, moving

them rhythmically, and tracing a shape similar to the uneven spirals drawn on the walls, which seemed to now resonate. His eyes imbued a shade of glowing ochre to match the canopy of golden roots that adorned the grotto. He jibbered inaudibly, but his words steadily grew louder. "Elvu'bakal, n'cha, kantu- Ta'halmuk! Thalmak! Shub, n'cha, Thalmak!" The chant waxed with increasing frenzy, and the professor's hands swirled with frenetic chaos. It seemed like a great shudder shot through the tree, which began a wavy and shifting movement, becoming animated. The upper branches of the tree began severing from the multitudes of connected roots, like a body suddenly pulling free from intravenous fluid cables like those used for cholera patients. Its lower body separated and violently sundered into four legs, taking a quadrupedal stance. The upper body's numerous branching limbs flailed sporadically, as if each had their own lifeforce. The extensive, tangled, and writhing mass of countless branches looked more like tentacles in their fluid bending and movement. A great shiver seized hold of Roger's whole body at the sight. With each passing moment, the thing resembled less of a tree and more like some ancient monster that had woken from dormancy.

The creature was fully free, its dark shape a protest to Roger's reality as it lurched unnaturally. Roger was surprised there was enough room on that knoll for Reginald, who had backed away as far as the space would allow and seemed a little unsure himself of his footing. "The corrupted child of the Black Goat of the Woods, the finger of Thalmak, malformed, altered, powerful," Reginald said, with reverence. "Only rarely is such nourishment brought to the charnel trough" he added, with relish. He turned his head and mouthed some words, whispering a secret entreaty to the horrid beast, then turned to Roger with malice, pointing out a slender finger. "Devour him!"

The monster dived into the pool of the grotto and swiftly swam to close the distance across the small pool towards Roger, cutting through the water like a knife. Roger struggled to understand how a creature without any noticeable eyes could navigate, and then he heard a strange ringing sound emit from it that filled the whole grotto. With each great movement, all of its tentacles reached forward and stroked in perfect unison. Snapping himself from shock, Roger began running to the side, circumnavigating the edge of the pool, but he kept his eyes on Reginald. The professor looked very pale in this light, and appeared to be wheezing deep breaths, his veins protruding. *Summoning that fiend exerted him greatly. I'd like to hope that the wounds he took earlier this night weren't entirely without consequence!* Roger calculated that he had some chance against this nightmare if he could neutralize the professor. Yet Reginald stood upon the rise at the far end of the pool, which meant that Roger would have to somehow cross the water, all the while being susceptible to both threats. Roger's only option was desperate chance. The moment the creature surfaced out of the water onto Roger's side of the grotto, he raised his shotgun at Reginald and immediately fired both barrels. Roger didn't even look to see the effect of his shot and cast aside the gun as he dove into the pool.

Roger swam with desperate fury. His clothes encumbered him, dragging at his motion as they soaked with water. He clutched the dagger from Eugene in his right fist but had nothing else. There was a splash in the water nearby; the creature was pursuing him. The mound was already just out of arm's reach, but immediately he felt something coiling around his legs, painfully jerking him back. He turned about, as more of the tentacles lashed out at him, constraining him. His buoyancy was disrupted by this, his head bobbing below and above the surface as he coughed when water filled his mouth. Sight and sound were muddled with his disrupted balance, but he could make out how such a creature could consume its quarry. Where no maw had been apparent before, Roger saw at the end of each and every tentacle, there was a vicious mouth with tiny sharp teeth, gnashing wildly. The ones that did not attack him were open, creating the insufferable, screeching chorus. Some of the jaws had already found their mark and clasped onto him, biting through his drenched clothes, which provided some barrier against the myriad pricks of sharp pain that tore at his flesh. The area of water by the maws felt hot, and Roger's blood stained the tenebrous currents of the pool. A shadow crossed his mind at the utter terror of being consumed in such a way, which was only overwhelmed by instinct and pain.

Through some miracle his right hand was not yet constrained, perhaps as it was further away from the direction of the creature's attacks. He lashed out at the tentacles with the dagger, striking each time he felt the sting of a biting mouth. In this manner he did not even need to see his target, disoriented as he was, flailing about in the water. Roger had never counted himself as a strong man, but the dagger had an intrinsic, flowing deftness in its design, and was weightless in the water. Even with his strikes slowed by submersion, the dagger cleaved through liquid and tentacles alike without difficulty and severed them instantly. This stirred the shrieking to an even higher frequency that bombarded Roger's ears, causing them to bleed. The remaining tentacles withdrew, buying Roger a moment's reprieve. He placed the handle of the dagger between his teeth, ignoring the pain from the mosaic of bites.

Roger reached up, his hands grasping at the patchy turf of the raised mound. He nearly pulled himself up, but faltered, his left hand slipping on the smooth, wet stone, and his body lowered back into the water. At that same moment, Roger felt a great blast of heat and pressure wash over from above. He felt a searing pain on the back of his right hand, which still clutched the ledge. He squinted to see that large patches of the skin of his backhand had been scorched right off, while the flesh that remained was burned. *I was a slip from being incinerated.* Roger grew faint, his vision blurring for a moment as he clung to consciousness. Had it not been for the great horror in the water with him, he likely would have succumbed. Instead, with a wailing and desperate yawp, he pulled himself onto the hill.

The professor reclined on the mound. Roger's shotgun blast had apparently found its mark, and Reginald's chest was bleeding. The patches of visible skin displayed some of the signature pockmark wounds from a shotgun's buckshot, but the wounds already seemed to have closed unnaturally by yellowish membranes. He looked like he had aged twenty years since Roger had first knocked on his door earlier that night. It looked like it took all of Reginald's strength to keep from toppling flat onto his back, and Roger could see prominent streaks of white in Reginald's long hair. His whole body was trembling—save his teeth, which were locked together, the foundation of a stare saturated with seething. The net effect made Reginald's handsome features look warped and demonic in the dim yellow light. At the sight of Roger, he outstretched his hand, his palm open and fingers spread wide, the same motion he had done numerous times before drawing on that dark power that eviscerated all matter. The motion had brought a part of the professor's body within reach of Roger, who thrusted the odd dagger forward, piercing straight through the center of the vulnerable palm.

Reginald howled in pain as his kicking legs scrambled his whole body backward, bloodily freeing his impaled hand. "You fool!" He spat the words, and Roger could still hear him, despite the ringing in his ears. "I cannot appeal to it in such a state! You will have unleashed a great hell on all your friends!" He shifted his movement and abruptly lunged toward Roger. Roger dropped the dagger and could only brace himself, throwing both of his hands up as his back squared to the ground. His emergence from the pool had made not only him slick, but also the ground beneath. The force of the professor's lunge and the sudden lack of a target sent him flying over Roger, who pushed up with all his remaining strength as Reginald passed over him. He was launched past Roger and sent careening into the pool with an echoing splash. The creature was alarmed at this and writhed for some time at the spot where Reginald had disappeared under the water. With this distraction, Roger prepared to jump from the small island directly to the closest shore of the cavern floor. He threw off his soaked and tattered shoes, picked the dagger back up, and got as much of a running start in his wet stockings as the space allowed. He leaped over the pool and cleared it.

Roger ran and did not look back, following the weak stream and trusting Reginald's comment that it would eventually join up with the Fox River. The cave narrowed so that Roger had to run directly through the frigid stream, and his feet further protested at running along the hard, rocky floor. The headroom was dwindling, and the gleam from the roots vanished along with their presence. Roger skimmed his uninjured hand along the sloping, earthen ceiling to guide him as it became too dark, and he reserved some hope that the space would become too small for the creature to pass through. He thought to himself, *soon it could amount to almost no space at all. The water only needs a sliver of space for a stream of this size to join up with the Fox. I could be trapped in a dead end like Shepard, gnawed away until I'm insane, or dead.* He could hear it now, pursuing in the distance, thrashing through the water. A draft of fresh air kissed Roger from ahead, and he could see a dim light at the end of the tunnel.

Roger got down on his belly into the frigid stream, his body shocked by the icy water. He grimaced and scraped along the stony bed. As his hands grasped forward, his right hand winced in pain at the cold moisture on the exposed flesh. Suddenly, he found the water became much deeper as he fully submerged, and his watery path gave way to the greater depths of the Fox River. He made a determined stroke upward, and he emerged to see the firmament above, resplendent with stars. It was a beautiful sight after the purgatory in the tunnels of Haunchyville. Already, the sky was touched with a cold grayness, the very first yielding to the coming dawn. A good swimmer, Roger directed himself toward the shoreline and pulled himself up onto the turf of the southern bank. He finally had a moment to breathe, but his teeth chittered since he felt even colder, his whole body shaking. It dawned on him how thirsty he was, and he bent himself over the flowing water, clasping his hands to collect precious draughts, as he had lost his flask in the tunnels. Roger surveyed the surrounding countryside of fescue, low hills, and farmland which looked unknown, yet somehow familiar. At least it was now a simple matter to return to the city; he could walk along the river, going upstream. He turned to examine the way from which he had come, but in the dim light he found it was nearly impossible to discern where the small underground stream joined up. The river itself was about forty feet wide here, and he silently reserved hope that the creature would not follow and that the opening would be too small to permit it through. *Perhaps the creature is bound to that place by an incantation of Linden's or restricted by some aspect of its damnable existence.*

Roger's hopes proved ill-founded. The creature must have been very dexterous, or could shape its body to a tremendous degree, for Roger could see the infernal, flailing appendages of the entity lashing the surface of the water. It seemed larger now, walking upright and bipedally, unrestrained by the confines of the grotto and surging to its full height—an abominable shape that continued to barrage Roger's sanity. For a moment, he collapsed, grasping the turf, and he dug his fingers into the yielding soil. His breaths were choked as he trembled through weeping palpitations. This arcane horror was not an insanity confined to the separate world he had just left behind, with dwarf men and strange roots which did God knows what to his faculties. This creature was just as real as Roger's dinner he had had that evening, as his bed where he would rest his head each night, as the swirling emotions that kindled in his heart for Lucy. It shambled towards him and screeched, perhaps only fifty feet away. Roger willed himself again to his feet. He could have collapsed on that turf, and his body would not protest. Not even his instinct could persist forever in moving his aching muscles.

But something internal and unidentifiable still demanded that he run. To the southwest, he could run in the path that the river flowed, which would likely lend speed to the creature. He would pass by some farms and lead it away from the city, eventually to be devoured when his strength failed. Running north would usher the danger back to his friends and the people of Waukesha. He was unsure of how far away he was, but his odds were better of reaching the city before his strength would finally be exhausted. Heading south was death; heading north was uncertainty, yet what dismal hope remained found better shelter that way. What else did he have other than his instincts when each moment demanded action? Roger would trust his feelings as he counted them as the last thing that would betray him, when all other senses and reason would fail.

7

The abomination was fast. Roger felt that he was moving very swiftly, perhaps faster than he ever had moved. While Roger's sides burned, and his throat dried up, he did not slacken his pace. Despite this, the creature was ever near, lunging and heaving through the river, although while Roger forced this pace, the threat grew neither closer nor more distant. Roger's mind was playing out how his last stand would go, but then he noticed a structure looming ahead. There was some type of manufacturing plant on the north side of the river, a looming silhouette of a brick building from which a pair of smokestacks rose. A mounted sign of metal paneling declared the identity of the business: EVERS AUTOMATION. There were two above-ground copper pipes, large enough for a man to crawl through and showing signs of oxidation, that apparently discharged directly to the river. Although they were not spewing anything now, there was a visible pool of a cloudy, pollutant substance in the immediate vicinity near the pipes, that resisted the natural flow of the river. Only at the opposite shore of the river did the water continue flowing by in a narrow streak, unafflicted. Roger could have cried out with joy at the sight of civilization, repulsive and crude as it was. His attention was redirected to another sight—an approaching party on the same side of the river, coming toward him.

Sam River was at the front of the group, carrying a hatchet and a glowing lantern. Sam warily regarded the wretch who shuffled toward him, but then cried out in alarm as the figure buckled and toppled over, just feet from the river. The group caught up to Roger, who had collapsed just across from the manufacturing plant near the polluted pool in the river. Roger's eyes looked vacant, and they drifted slowly to regard Sam. The others kneeled down around him. Roger became dimly aware of Sam, Peaches, someone he did not know, and then his vision wheeled into clarity as his eyes focused on the last member of the group, Lucy Morris. "Lucy!" Roger rasped, "No! It's too dangerous here. All of you, it's coming—"

"Shh . . . it's all right now." Lucy interrupted, setting aside a lantern and gently bearing up Roger's head and resting it on her lap. "Goodness, you're cold. Were you in the water?" Roger managed a nod, and Lucy then looked up, peering downriver, and sighted the thing that Roger had warned them about. A striding menace surged through the water with a relentless fury. It emitted a high frequency screeching noise and had numerous, writhing tentacles, springing like branches from its oily trunk. Lucy's widened eyes already hardened into a petrified stare. "You all can see that, right? That . . . thing?"

"Y-yes, mam," Peaches replied through stifled speech,

listlessly tapping his baseball bat against the ground. "I was hoping it might have just been in my head too. Sweet Jesus, it would have been better off just staying there!" he whimpered, and lowered the bat to lean against it as he took uneven breaths while avoiding looking at the creature directly.

"This old Earth has many spirits, benevolent and malignant. But I have not seen anything like this outside of tale and song. What times are these, that such a thing walks freely?" Sam asked, grimly. "It's moving too fast . . ."

"It's coming closer! Bless my waking eyes, it's upon us! But I . . . I have my duty to uphold," the other man, a uniformed police officer added, raising his service pistol at the approaching horror. "You'll need to move your friend, Roger, quickly!"

Roger still shivered terribly but discovered he still had some reserve strength so that Lucy and Peaches were able to support him as he hobbled further upstream and away from the outreaching tentacles. Lucy, surprised by Roger's resilience, questioned him. "I know I said to rest, but this creature—can it only move in the water?"

"No, it can move on dry land, too. I had been following the river, looking for help. I don't know if it's susceptible to anything. It's some horror awoken by the professor. He drew power from it."

Lucy and Peaches had taken Roger some thirty feet away from the river and gently set him back down. Peaches took off his jacket and got it onto Roger before running back to the fray. Lucy poured some water from a bottle into Roger's mouth and over his lips and quickly kissed him on the forehead. She then returned with Peaches to Sam and the officer, who were trying to hold the creature at bay. The officer had shot it several times and was fumbling nervously while trying to reload his weapon. A tentacle lashed at his arm, and with a spray of blood the pistol was flung clear into the river. Sam stood on the precipice of the water's edge, making flourishing strikes with his axe as his long hair whirled with his movements. He succeeded in severing a couple of the tentacles, but also took injuries of attrition where he was lashed at or bit by the gnashing maws at the tentacles' ends. A sudden burst of heat scorched Sam's brown suede jacket, which he threw to smolder on the turf. "I can't keep this up!" Sam yelled. Peaches charged with his bat and began bashing the trunk of the creature in a frenzy, while hysterically shifting to avoid the creature's attacks.

"Well, it looks like a tree, so why don't we try burning it?" Lucy bellowed.

"It's in a river, honey!" Peaches offered as diplomatically as possible as he desperately put his weight into each blow of his weapon. He readied another swing, and his willow bat shattered upon impacting the creature's body, leaving Peaches only with the sundered handle and blistered hands as he ran back.

"We could try to lure it away!" Sam shouted, wincing in pain as he slashed yet another tentacle away that had latched onto him.

"Wait, that sludge in the water, it could slow it down at least!" Lucy cried out, pointing to the dark, scummy surface on the section of the river.

"It's worth a chance! We cannot outlast it," the officer agreed, clubbing at the entity and then retreating along the river's shoreline. The monster pursued the officer, who baited it right to the edge of the polluted area. Suddenly the creature withdrew its attacking tentacles, submerging them all into the water. The officer held his ground as the others came around, positioning themselves at a bend in the river, which angled the turbid tarn directly between them and the monster. A great spout of boiling water issued forth from underneath the beast at great speed, blasting the unsuspecting man, who howled out in pain as he fell to the ground. Peaches prepared to rush out to help him, but an arm checked him—Sam River's. "No! Peaches, you can't!" Sam rebuked. "Not yet! We need to lure it into the roily pool first, he added, his eyes darting back to the oil lantern Lucy held, and then to his own. "We can't risk it chasing after you instead!"

Yet at the moment the creature's form would have coursed into the pool to move nearer to its prey, it halted, perhaps sensing the danger, and began to circumnavigate the area, creeping back towards the shore. Lucy threw her lantern at a tussock on the bank where the beast was approaching, and it reeled back, screeching at the sudden burst of flame as the oil lantern exploded among the reeds, spreading out. It halted momentarily, but still turned and moved away from the pool in another direction. "No!" Lucy cried out. She threw off her coat and ran forward leaping directly into the pulpy wastewater. She emerged out of the grime, wheezing for a moment and opening her eyes, white diamonds against the dark smudge that covered her. "Come get me you ugly bastard!"

This provocation worked, and the creature bolted towards her, surging faster than they had yet witnessed. "Good God, no!" Peaches cried out, and this time Sam had difficulty restraining him, nearly dropping his lantern in the process. "It's moving too fast! I have to get her out of there!"

"She's made up her mind, Peaches! We can't waste this chance she's given us! Just wait!"

"To Hell with that! It should be me in that damned river!"

Again, Peaches jostled with Sam, who hit Peaches hard on the back of his head, stunning him. The creature entered the pool, its tentacles, dripping with sludge, lunged out toward their prey. Sam threw his lantern true with a sweeping, underhanded loft. It shattered against the trunk of its body, just above the water. A great blaze whirled up in the twinkling of an eye, fueled by the oily water. The shrieking noise from the myriad mouths reached a deafening level and echoed throughout the prairie. The small inferno greedily enveloped the creature's body, as if the flames were attracted to expelling the entity. Folding layers of flesh effused in weeping spurts, but still the horror jerked and twisted to escape the pool. At last, the sound of the maws ceased, replaced by the whistle of burgeoning flame as the very surface of the water caught fire. The swollen polyps on the branches burst, exuding the strange milk inside, nourishing the fire to fan out even more swiftly across the polluted surface.

Lucy screamed as she desperately tried to swim out of the muck. Her movements were panicked and hindered by the halting substance of the wastewater. Only seconds after Sam had thrown his lantern, nearly the whole width of the river had become ablaze. He scrambled to close the distance to Lucy while Peaches recovered. The fire was licking at the heels of her rubber boots, and she had nearly fought her way back to the bank of the river. But by now she was fighting to keep herself from drowning, disoriented and weighed down by the grimy water. She gasped and choked on some of the vile fluid, and she could feel the flames licking at her legs. Her courage began to break down as she faced death. In a final desperate gesture, she reached out an arm in vain, clutching blindly in repeated motion at nothing, just feet from the bank.

Sam managed to grab hold of her arm and pulled. He struggled and nearly slid in himself, until another hand reached out and caught hold of him. Roger had managed to crawl over to join the rescue effort, and with a spurt of strength, the duo at last pulled her from the suction of the flaming sludge onto the river bank. Lucy's teeth jittered and was covered with icy filth, but apart from her boots, she had been marvelously unharmed. She looked at Roger, the low eastern sun behind him on the horizon, sporting a wan smile in between wheezes. After mustering this, he rocked backward, passing out on the slope of the riverbank. He could vaguely feel the warmth of a sunbeam touching his face, then his mind went dark.

Roger awoke to discover that he was inside of the patient ward at a hospital. He was in a comfortably fixed bed, propped up on several pillows. His vision was blurry, and he found that a cool towel rested on his forehead. As his vision returned, he looked to see other empty beds in the ward, but he noticed that a few were occupied. He felt a dull pain on the back of his hand and discovered that it was heavily bandaged. With the return of sensation Roger became increasingly aware of of painful spots over his body. Overcoming his discomfort, he called out as loud as he could. "Nurse! Sister? Please, help me! Do you have a telephone here? Perhaps a telegraph?"

Deaconess Mary Krause, who had been responsible for Roger's care, informed him that he was in Passavant Hospital in Milwaukee, and that his belongings had been brought over by some friends from his previous accommodations in Waukesha. Deaconess Krause had taken the courtesy to notify that same group of friends who had insisted on being contacted the moment Roger woke up, and he brought out his notepad and materials while he waited for them to arrive. He did this before realizing that he, of course, could no longer write with his right hand. He was told by Dr. Meyer, who checked on him a short time later, that he could do so again in time, with proper healing. The doctor's greatest fear of pneumonia setting in had passed, as Roger's core body temperature had risen to nearly normal, with no other worrisome symptoms. Roger found his folder with his three articles that he had intended to submit to the *Tribune*: *Waukesha Springs House Primes for Resurgent Holiday Season, Ho-Chunk Powwows and Bridging Communities, and Elusive Haunchyville*. Roger laughed dryly at how inappropriate they had become, apart from the article on the Ho-Chunk, which would require no alterations. It seemed like he had written them weeks ago, and it dawned on him that he did not know how long he had been resting as he regarded the eastern sun.

Roger recalled setting out with Linden on the night of Tuesday, the twentieth of October, and those events had extended into the wee hours of Wednesday morning. Roger was subsequently notified that it was 10:30 in the morning on October the twenty-third, and that he had been resting for nearly forty-eight hours since he was brought to Milwaukee. He had missed his deadline to submit the stories in time for today's edition and wondered if he would still have a job. He insisted on changing out of the hospital gown into his own clothes and later was helped over to one of the hospital's three telephones to contact Lou.

"Holy Christ, you're alive!" Lou exclaimed after Roger's greeting. "I was beginning to think you ran off to join the *Sentinel!* Where the Hell are you?"

"I suffered some injuries while in the field . . . I've been at Passavant Hospital in Milwaukee. I think I shall be well enough to return later today," Roger said and turned to the Deaconess, who gave him a withering scowl. "Or tomorrow."

Roger posited his return times as timidly as he could in his drowsy state, but considered it progress that he had not already been informed of his termination.

"Injuries? What in the . . . never mind. Roger, Roger, I can't begin to explain to you how slow it's been. We had to put out eight community pieces today! Eight! All of our readers are now well-acquainted with Lyle Connor's budding interest in lepidopterology to Agnes Zielinski's Golabki recipe. Would you like me to tell you what goes in a proper Golabki dish, Roger?"

"I'll be able to make up for my absence, Lou, I promise. I did get some material for my trouble here. I hope you'll give me the chance," he concluded, unable to rouse an impassioned appeal in his state.

There was a pause, and then finally Lou spoke again. "I'll give you more than a chance, Roger. I'm very interested to see how your materials have shaped up, but you better be here soon. That hospital bill is your responsibility, by the way—but *I'm* the one who's dying without you, Roger . . . dying! My office! Tomorrow afternoon! I'll come in on a bloody Saturday! Perhaps we can salvage Monday's edition," he added under his breath, not exactly to Roger. "Can you manage that?"

"I'll see you then, Lou."

Roger returned to his bed, still wobbly and faint, but feeling something of an appetite stirring within. The recovering journalist further resolved to get out of the hospital as soon as possible after being served a horrid dish of porridge and an odd meat-pudding. He would need to dictate his draft to someone in order to be ready to face Lou Baker tomorrow. Roger felt overwhelmed when he considered his full list of things that he needed to get done. Around one o'clock in the afternoon Roger received his visitors. He sat up a little more and smiled to see his "usual suspects," Lucy, Peaches, and Sam. There were warm salutations, and Roger received a pat on the shoulder from Peaches, while Lucy kissed him on the check and tenderly embraced him.

Roger was able to start with his questions first, and learned he wasn't the only person who had spent time recovering. They all had suffered some injuries, each sporting various bandages. Peaches had developed diminished hearing, perhaps permanently, and Lucy was kept for half a day at the hospital after her time in the river, but fortunately had fully mended from chills and minor burns. Next, Roger wished to know the identity and status of the policeman who had been with them. Sam told him that he was a man by the name of Adam Lombard, who had fortunately survived and was on the slow path of recovering from second and third-degree burns. Finally, Roger had asked how he happened on them at the river. It turned out that Peaches came looking for Roger a couple hours after their discovery at the Spring House and reading the note that Roger had left for him at the hotel. By this point in the evening, the police had already contacted and informed Lucy of the tragic business at the Spring House.

"My sleep for the night had been ruined after hearing

about my dear Cynthia," Lucy said with a quivering lip at mentioning her departed friend, and she took a moment before resuming. "At times she would stay late, like that night. I think sometimes she and her fiancé would use the bar, or the baths. The pay is so humble, I thought I was doing her a favor. She was probably waiting for him, but instead . . ." she paused to recollect herself. "After I had come by and spoken with the authorities, I found Peaches skulking about outside of the Spring House, just outside of the police presence with the letter from you. We resolved that we weren't going to let you and the professor do all of the investigating. It probably worked out better that you went off first. I doubt your chivalry would have permitted your agreement for me to accompany you on such a venture."

Both Peaches and Roger protested this last statement— Roger at the knowledge that his chivalry was well-intentioned, even justified, and Peaches at the implication that teaming up with Lucy reflected his lack of such a quality. This brought a small smile to Lucy's lips, who did not seem wearied by the display. "It's all right boys. You both were doing right by your own conscience. Didn't I already say that it worked out for the best?"

That quieted the interruption. Lucy continued with the narration that she had obtained Reginald Linden's address from her copy of the city directory that she possessed for mailing new and returning guests of the Spring House. Things became more difficult for them when they found the professor's residence locked and vacated. There was a discussion then to go home for the night or to speculate where Roger and Reginald would investigate. "It's not a glamorous way to go about things, hoping that you can guess the mind of someone," Lucy said, smiling with the subtle judgment of Roger's decision-making of that night. "But then Peaches and I agreed that we ought to at least check with Sam before conceding defeat. It was certainly a shot in the dark."

The on-foot journey out to Sam's residence at that time of night was not an easy one. Peaches had been conditioned for long stretches in the cold because he played ball. Lucy explained that the outfit she used for wading through the shallows of springs pools for her monthly inspections during the busy season (complete with tall, custom-made water-resistant boots) made it more tolerable than she had anticipated.

"I was surprised to see the late visitors," Sam began. "Although I was not startled, as I was already on edge from what sounded like distant gunshots about half an hour earlier. That's uncommon when it isn't deer hunting season. At any rate, I figured their visit might have had something to do with you, as was the case," he said, addressing Roger. "At that point I realized we would need some luck to track you down. My only guess was that you knew the whereabouts of Thomas Moss's residence. He wasn't the sort to stay in one spot long enough to be included in the city directory, and I didn't know where he lived either, so that seemed like it would be the end of it. But my mind returned to those shots

I had heard, and then I was the one who couldn't sit still. I knew that Evers had his plant northeast of my plot further upriver. I had to make sure that he didn't have you in some kind of danger over there. Besides, if you get lost in this area, the best thing you can do is find the Fox and follow it back to the city."

"That was precisely my line of thought!" Roger offered happily.

The group had then gone to the river and encountered the Sheriff, Adam Lombard. Lombard had been patrolling the premises in response to incessant watch-requests filed by Evers to the police of nightly vandalism on his plant's outbuildings. The sheriff was happy enough to join the group to search for their missing friend and together they patrolled along the Fox for more than hour. As it turned out, they were on their last leg before giving it up when they had spotted Roger running frantically towards them. "But that's enough of that!" Peaches spoke up. "We've given you the courtesy of telling our rather uninteresting night first, given your condition, but now it's time for you to tell us what you uncovered with the professor. We were half-expecting he'd turn up now to check on you," Peaches explained.

Roger breathed deeply, and then began his account, holding nothing back from his close friends. He told them of his confusion at the discovery at the Spring House and his desire to find a clear suspect. It dawned on Roger too late of the professor's involvement and bore witness to the fantastic and horrifying power that he wielded against the lowlifes. "I still don't have the faintest idea how he calls on such invisible powers. He held death in his very hands, exploding the air itself. He has some exceptionally old and decrepit books. I surmise there could be some method or instruction in those ancient texts, if one had a lifetime and command of dozens of languages. He either had special genius or made some dark pact to wade through them, or both. I only got the smallest of glances when interviewing him. It would be quite the coup to have a closer look at his collection."

Roger began his strangest tale about how he fled into the forest and stumbled upon the mythical Haunchyville. It was here that he received the most questions and interruptions, mainly from Peaches. "Little vicious dwarf people? Come off it! What kind of foolish name is Haunchyville anyway? Sounds like a circus act that got forgotten about and left in the woods! You didn't see an overturned *Ringling Brothers* wagon anywhere, did you?"

Peaches's curiosity was not satisfied until Roger provided a vivid description of his encounter, which included a clarification that technically he only had a second-hand account that the dwarves were vicious. Roger continued recounting his flight from the professor through the tunnels under the gnarled trees. "I should have obtained more of that root sample for a botanist, or a . . . dendrologist, I think is the word. I wonder if it's unique to only those tunnels?"

"Enough about the sodding trees! Were there more little people?" Peaches asked.

Roger continued, sharing his discovery of the haunchymen

in the tunnels and a dying Eugene Shepard. Peaches contained his ceaseless excitement as Roger emotionally recounted his exchange with the man. "I would like to go back, if I could. Shepard wanted me to share his story, but I don't know how I can, apart from with the three of you. I owe my survival to him—" Roger abruptly cut himself off. His thoughts turned to the strange dagger gifted to him by Shepard. He had completely forgotten about it until just now. "They told me that you moved my things over for me from the hotel. Did you find a strange little dagger?"

At this, Sam nodded and reached into his trouser pocket and carefully produced the item. "I was mighty curious about this, and I don't get that way easily, mind you. I thought the hospital staff might confiscate this if they found such a sharp little knife on you, so I thought that I'd hang onto it for safekeeping." Sam winked and stepped forward, looking from side to side for approaching staff, and then set it in Roger's non-bandaged hand.

"Shepard found it somewhere in the caves," Roger said, distractedly, closely re-examining the weapon. "It's the darndest thing. It served me very well. It has sort of an odd beauty, don't you think?"

The others agreed very quietly and hesitantly, and Roger sensed that they were taken aback at his charmed opinion of the dagger. He set it aside and picked up with his descent to the grotto of the strange tree where he once again encountered Reginald Linden. "He spoke a very strange incantation, probably from what he believed to be the forgotten language

167

of his lost tribe. It animated that thing . . . I do not wish to keep calling it a tree . . . well, you all caught a glimpse of it, name it what you wish. I was able to scrape by it, fending off its attacks with this," he said, once again raising the dagger. "Reginald tried to use that same magic to kill me, but my own clumsiness saved me." Roger raised his bandaged hand. "It's funny now that I think about it. We both wounded each other's right hand. I stabbed him when he reached out. I wonder if there's something in the Bible about that? Leviticus?" He shook his head, refocusing. "Yet I did not kill him. He fell into the spring in the grotto after reaching out for me. That's when I began my escape. There was a little stream from that spring that feeds into the Fox, and that's how I was able to get out. I believe that creature must have killed Reginald. I did see it writhing over the spot in the water that he had fallen. He was also severely injured and spent by that point . . ."

Roger's voice had been trailing off. Sam looked at him grimly, and Roger understood that they both shared the realization that was apparent from Roger's account. "I must admit, it's possible that he's still alive." A silence in the room followed, and the window of the hospital room suddenly creaked loudly with a gust of autumnal wind. "I thought that I would inevitably be outpaced by the creature, but I . . ." Roger could not hold back his tears. His management of his complex emotions and battered sanity was faltering as he looked up at his friends. He reached up with his left hand, rubbing underneath his eyes. "But then I found my saviors!"

Lucy sat down on the bed, comforting him as he rested his head against her bosom, slowly coming back from that memory. The accounts had been shared, and the great burden of the communal trauma and nightmares could now be faced with solidarity. "I would be dead or a wreck were it not for all of you! Lucy, I think we were all outdone by your heroism, especially."

"Hey, you deserve some credit too, pal," Peaches rebuked. "I guess there's some hero in everybody when the time calls for it, like being up with runners on in the ninth!" This evoked a laugh from the group, who were satisfied with (although likely not properly understanding) Peach's closing remark to avoid more gushing affirmations. "That thing took a while to burn up, I should mention," Peaches added further. "You didn't really get a good show of it after you collapsed. By the end, it was difficult to discern where polluted water or remnants began, the whole surface had thickened up."

"But I suppose we've left a terrible mess from a legal standpoint." Roger drudged up the unpleasant point. "They likely won't start any investigation on Linden, at least not right away, but that leaves the two victims at the Spring House, and also the three men from the field. Jim Smitheran and the ox-faced man . . . I don't suppose I know what happened to the other fellow. I squared him good in the face, but I didn't kill him. I hope the professor didn't—there was no need for that. But even still, that's at least four dead, an officer seriously injured, and one missing. Two if you count Shepard!"

"We've had a considerable amount of help in that, it seems," Sam said. "That fellow who you knocked out in the field? His name is Steffen Bundy. He was taken in for questioning by the Milwaukee Police, who have taken over the investigation. I don't know if he's telling things as straight as you are right now, but I feel like you might receive a visit from the detective if this fellow implicated you in anything. With some luck, he might even feel some gratitude toward you, on account of your . . . non-lethal takedown."

"As for the Spring House," Lucy took her turn to explain, "I sat down with Detective Ferguson. He's satisfied that you and Peaches had nothing to do with what went on there. Fred Mueller vouched for the two of you during the suspected time of the murder, and they didn't find any implicating evidence. It looks like for better or for worse, the blame for these murders is being connected between Moss and those other two from the field. They all had histories, and one even had an outstanding warrant for his arrest before any of this occurred. Finally, we have the account that Adam Lombard is offering. He's recovering at this same hospital, and he's regained his ability to speak. We've heard he's been recounting that we helped him out of quite a scrape. I think he called it an industrial accident and a pack of ravenous coyotes." Lucy paused, momentarily. "He might even remember things that way. It's hard to speculate how a person's mind reconciles such trauma. I still see that thing burned into my mind," she finished, just above a whisper.

That satisfied Roger's worries for the time, and they all

proceeded to exchange mailing addresses, and Sam was the first to excuse himself with a gracious goodbye. A shadow crept over Roger's mind as he watched Sam exit. He thought that Sam may have a mind to check on Haunchyville and the fate of the professor, and either would be a dark road for one man to brave. "Sam, you take care of yourself," Roger said as Sam nodded back to him.

Peaches informed Roger that he, too, intended to head back to Chicago to begin his winter employment. Roger surprised him with another job opportunity for the next couple of days as his transcriber, which he happily accepted. Peaches left to secure a train to Chicago for the next morning and told Roger he would be back in a couple of hours to begin working. That left just Roger and Lucy in the room. "Please keep an eye on Sam for me," Roger began. "He knew Reginald the longest of any of us, and I think this turn of events has been especially hard on him, even if he doesn't show it."

"I think he knows better than to feel responsible for those impossibly hidden machinations," Lucy began quietly, holding Roger's uninjured hand between hers. "But I'll be there for him if he wants someone to talk to. I suppose that's better than nothing, when your concept of a friend has been shattered. As for the two of us, this is farewell then?"

"God, I hope not," Roger said, looking up at her intently. "Hopefully just 'until next time.' But I'm afraid I must return to Chicago if I wish to keep my employment."

"You should, then. I hope they're not too hard on you."

She turned her focus away from Roger, now looking to one of the windows, which admitted the remnant of the evening's light. "It's funny, carrying on a secret like this between a few people. If we went out and shared what we all experienced, we would probably be interred at an asylum. It's as if there's not enough room in this world, for accounts like that . . . people have already made up their minds about what they'll accept. As for us, we just need to carry on like nothing has happened. There's something so horrid and unfair about it!" She finished, faltering and beginning to tear up.

Roger quickly sat upright and placed a supportive arm around her shoulder. She seemed surprised to see such a movement out of him. "I'm not a damn invalid!" he joked, which got a laugh out of Lucy. "You think you have it bad, carrying on with what you know? I make a living sharing my perspective! I'm going to have a devil of a time framing my stories, but we'll make it, I'm sure of it. We've already been through the rough stuff, worse than what most people will ever have to go through."

Lucy took some comfort in that, and they continued their conversation very quietly, her head still resting on his shoulder. "I will be sad to see you leave," she said formally, standing up.

"Leaving you behind is dreadful for me. Will the Spring House survive? I may have to move here, and put my mixed feelings for some of its other denizens aside."

"Insurance is covering the wall damage. It's heads or tails as to what kind of effect all the rumors surrounding what happened will have on it. I suppose I'll be happy if I can keep it up and running for another year before the owners decide to close or sell it. I should be returning soon. I still have a job to do over there." She stood back up. "You promise to write me?"

"Of course. You might have to make me promise *not* to write, if I'm able to get back to my prodigious pace," he said boastfully, again sparking some laughter. He stood up and pulled her closer to him with his good hand, and they kissed. Lucy eventually broke away with, "Until next time," which conveyed to Roger all that he needed to know and more as he watched her graceful and lingering exit. She left.

8

Peaches had atrocious handwriting. Roger looked over the dictations for his new stories, and if he had not personally spoken them aloud just moments ago, he would have had great difficulty making them out. As it stood, he could still convey these to a typist, and he thanked his friend all the same. "I know my hand isn't too good," Peaches said, shyly. "It turns out I don't need to use my letters much nowadays."

"You did fine, my friend."

"Since this won't be in your story, I just want to check again with you . . . the thing we ran up against at the automation plant is dead, but it was part of some larger thing, still living underground?"

"Yes, if what Reginald said can be trusted. I'll be looking further into whatever I can find, but I'm sure it will be slow going. Part of my editor's job is ensuring that I do not have much time for idle pursuits."

Peaches nodded and rubbed his nose. "I remember finding tangles of roots all of the time when doing my tilling and planting chores for my folks growing up. I always assumed they were from the dead plants of yesteryear, but some of the thick ones ran deep, and I couldn't fathom where they had come from or connected. Quite a thought—thinking that any dead-looking tree or unidentifiable root is a reaching appendage of that thing," he finished with a shudder.

"You booked us a train for tomorrow?"

"Yeah, we've got a 10:10 a.m. departure time. I hope that works out with your boss and everything."

"That will work perfectly. I will meet you at the station house."

"What? No breakfast?!" Peaches looked shocked, duplicating his expression when they had confronted the creature.

"Well, we can get breakfast, but it will have to be early. I have one last piece of business to take care of before we leave Milwaukee," Roger replied with resolution.

"You're sure you're fit enough to be running around tending to 'business?' I normally wouldn't balk at what a man wants to do on his own time, but we've had some formidable run-ins lately. I'll warn you, I'm all out of baseball equipment!"

"It won't be anything like that, Peaches. Just wrapping things up. I would appreciate having you with me, though. Dress . . . respectfully."

Peaches agreed to the request, and the two arranged to meet at a breakfast diner on Wells Street at seven-thirty the next morning. Peaches excused himself again and Roger had his meager hospital dinner. Afterwards, the Deaconess came by to change the bandages on his hand. Roger grimaced, both from the pain and the sight of the discolored skin on his hand. "It looks dreadful dear, I know," Deaconess

Krause remarked. "But it's certainly starting to heal. This new wrapping will last for another two days. The doctor said you may want them replaced at a hospital in Chicago, but at the very least have someone help you if you mean to do it yourself. You need to have it bandaged for at least one more week." Roger wondered if his hand would ever fully heal, but took comfort knowing that he would at least be able to leave the hospital in the morning.

After Deaconess Krause left, Roger proceeded to look over his two new transcripts which replaced his main article on the Springs House and the side story on the local curiosity of mythical Haunchyville. He had split and expanded his previous story into two: *Enduring Appeal: Waukesha's Fountain Spring House Here to Stay,* and *Spring City Terror: Four Dead as Drifter Brought to Justice!* The article on Haunchyville was removed; Roger had been hesitant on some of his decisions, but he was resolved against luring unsuspecting tourists and sightseers to that place, even if it were soon to become desolate. *There might be a time and place to bring the legend back, but it was not now.* Therefore, Roger archived the piece on Haunchyville, putting it aside. Still, he couldn't resist a strange inclination to mention the place's name once in *Spring City Terror* as one location of the deranged web of enigmatic sites of the prime suspect, Thomas Moss. Roger appraised the stories as the most riveting material that he had shared with the *Tribune* readers thus far. The journalist had walked a careful line with the perspective of the main story, providing as much detail as possible without altering what he knew about the testimony of his friends and others to the authorities. An unexpected opportunity to rest his remaining doubts presented itself when Roger received another visitor at eight o'clock that night. It was Detective Karl Ferguson of the Milwaukee Police Department.

Detective Ferguson had many of the signature elements of a Victorian man in appearance. He wore a gray waistcoat with an ascot visible under his collar. He had a bushy moustache and an uncompromising keenness to his stare, which remain fixed on Roger even while he removed his hat and sat down at a desk that had been pulled up beside the bed. "I recognize that you've been recovering from some considerable injuries and have spent most of the day resting, so I will be very brief, Mr. Merrick."

"It's no trouble, detective. I realize that you have to do your job, and preferably before all persons of interest are still in the area."

"Ah, good." The detective pulled out a notebook. "Now, I've pieced together an account of the events starting in the evening hours of Tuesday, October twentieth, through about 6:00 a.m. on Wednesday October twenty-first. I compiled this account from all of the known parties involved. Please tell me your version of the story. You may go as slowly as you like—I understand that this can be exhausting."

Roger handed him his transcribed story, *Spring City Terror: Four Dead as Drifter Brought to Justice!* "This account is precisely as it happened sir, from my point of view. In fact, I intend to share this with the good people of Chicago—the subscriber base of the *Tribune*, at least!"

"Well now, I get a preview! If that's how you'd prefer to do this then." The detective began reading then exclaimed, "By God, you make your living as a journalist with this kind of handwriting? Those poor typists!" He continued, occasionally writing some notes of his own upon spotting something of interest. His squint-eyed scanning and note-taking made the process much longer than a typical reading. At last, he handed the notebook back to Roger. "Very interesting . . . it's a good reflection on the local police, so I'm sure it will be well-received in Waukesha. Sensational, but not *sensationalized* as is often the case in the newspapers these days—if I dare to trust my own discernment." Detective Ferguson rose from his chair and paced over to the window, looking out at the night sky. "Officially, Mr. Merrick, I am satisfied, and it's for the best that I looked at that article before you published it. You seem to understand the delicacy of such stories. If it's any interest to you, the examiner concluded that Moss died of liquid poisoning, likely ingested with some tea or beverage. Fortunately, no conclusive link was made with the spring water, and let us pray that's true."

"Oh my," Roger said vacantly, thinking about his offered cup with Reginald that previous Sunday afternoon. "Does that conclude our business then, detective?" Roger asked, trying to mask any nervousness or impatience.

"As it concerns law and public safety, yes." He returned to his chair, but turned it around and sat down again, his crossed arms resting over the back of the chair. "It's skeletal evidence for all four deaths, and I don't think you are the man responsible for them. At times, a man in my position has to accept things settling on their own accord, when there's so little to work with. But unofficially, Officer Lombard told me that you had encountered a . . . monster outside of Evers Automation. Monster. I'd rather not send him to Mendota to have his mental state examined. What have you left out of your story? The condition that we found some of the bodies in as well . . . we squared things for the report, but in my eleven years as a detective, there are inconsistencies even with the appalling lack of hard evidence. I also saw the bizarre bite marks on your body while you were out, as well as the unusual burn pattern." He took out a pipe. "Do you mind?" Roger shook his head no, and the detective fussed with the tobacco for a moment and then proceeded to light it. "I'm not coming after you, but the others indicated, despite their best attempts to mask it, that you were in a better position to relate at least what happened in the field on Fred Mueller's property." There was now a little shroud of smoke hanging above the pensive man as he looked at Roger.

"All right, detective. Regarding what happened on Fred Mueller's property . . . I was with Mr. Reginald Linden at the time, oblivious to his interests in the occult. We were going to see if we could uncover answers from the news we had about the Spring House at Thomas Moss's cottage. We were assailed by three men who were apparently after Moss, a Jim Smitheran and two other fellows, one of whom I believe you talked with? Well, they threatened us with violence and robbery, and it was at this time that Linden used some . . . cantrips and hidden explosives through sleight of hand to rapidly dispatch the two men," said Roger, trying to balance his small assortment of lies in the story. "I fled from Linden after this sudden violence," Roger started up again to the attentive listener. "In doing so, I did eventually encounter something beyond the realm of normal explanation in that peculiar wood known as Haunchyville. This nameless horror pursued me to outside of the automation plant with my friends, which was responsible for Sheriff Lombard's and my own injuries. Certainly, the word monster fits the bill, difficult as it is to describe the shambling thing that was obscured in the low light. I can only say it was some impossible entity that had been corralled and summoned by Linden. We managed to burn the damn thing, and you can rest easier because of that. I apologize . . . I know it left nothing for forensic examination."

"There were a few reports of an unpleasant screeching noise," Detective Ferguson added to Roger, who nodded, confirming the connection. "What happened to this Linden, then?" he asked.

"I don't rightly know; the creature might have devoured him or left his body in some remote stretch of woods. If I had any inclination, I would try to lead you to the body, but I cannot recall. Please understand my position, Mr. Ferguson. My memory is clouded from the encounter, and these were things that simply cannot be said in the newspaper, for the benefit of the public. It's difficult enough relating what I experienced in an intelligible way, even to you. But that is the truth, such as it is."

Detective Ferguson hesitated and took a number of puffs from his pipe, turning his head to the side. It was a weary expression; evidently the man was digesting everything that Roger had said and written. The silence hung over the room like a dampened quilt. At length the detective rose, pushed the chair back in at the small table, and nodded at the recovering journalist. "Thank you, Mr. Merrick. That does satisfy my curiosity, for the most part. I understand your motivations, and for what it's worth, I believe you are telling the truth about what you witnessed. If you were lying, I don't think that you could have come up with a more unlikely story!" he added, with the hint of a smile. "I'm not exactly confident about how I will summarize my case file—it won't do to write, 'monster,' even if it was burned up. I don't suppose you saw a . . . what was it? A *Hodag*?" He stood and took a few paces away, and then lingered for a moment. "I've heard the name Haunchyville as well, though I can't place when. I've always found it a doleful and unpleasant name," he said aloud, not particularly to anyone. He gave a dry chuckle and left.

Roger anticipated fitful sleep that night. He had slept the better part of two days and was far from feeling tired. This would often be an industrious time to get work done, but the condition of his writing hand prevented that. He had arranged for a six-thirty wake-up call, blessedly without a breakfast provided, and had lain down in an attempt to sleep. Roger had not remembered dreaming during the last two nights, and he tossed and turned in his creaking hospital bed, avoiding putting pressure on his throbbing hand. Hours passed, and he became dimly aware of being caught in a dream-like state somewhere between waking and rest. He opened his eyes and saw a dark shape at his bedside, and a chill crept down his spine. The figure's outline matched one of the haunchy men who had somehow stalked him and now stooped next to him, staring in vigil.

Gasping at the sight, Roger lashed out at it with his left hand, which he suddenly realized had been clutching the dagger. The haunchy man vanished from Roger's delirious sight, and the force of his stab knocked over the chair of the side desk. The recoil shot down his arm with such intensity that it was as if the dagger had become an extended finger. In a sweat, Roger got up and set the weapon on the table next to his prepared stack of clothes for tomorrow when he noticed someone looking up at the disturbance from their bed further down the ward. Roger raised his hand to the onlooker reassuringly, and reached for the glass of water left for him by Deaconess Krause. After a drink he lay back down for another hour or so, all the while spying sinister and unseemly moving shapes throughout the ward, before finally drifting to sleep.

Roger was awakened by the Deaconess, and he bolted up with a start, in turn alarming the nurse. Following mumbled apologies, he dressed while the dim gray of morning filtered through the window. Roger left Passavant Hospital and carried the dagger in a large inner jacket pocket, wrapping a bit of spare bandage cloth along the blade to avoid poking himself during the day. The Wells Street Diner was a cozy and inviting place with a bustling crowd, and the featured breakfast for the day was hot muffins, choice of fried chicken or poached egg on toast, jelly, and tea or coffee. Roger and Peaches engaged in small talk while they had their beverages and awaited the food, greatly enjoying the respite from graver affairs. The food proved excellent, and Roger promised Peaches that he'd pick up the next meal as well as reimburse him for his ticket, as he was practically broke until he received his next advance from the *Tribune*.

Breakfast was concluded in less than an hour, and Roger and Peaches took a coach south, crossing the Milwaukee River at the bridge on Water Street. They arrived outside of St. Josaphat Church on Lincoln Avenue a little before nine o'clock. The church was certainly impressive, dominated by a massive dome of shining copper at its crown. Clocks were inlaid at the corners of the primary dome's supporting tower. The main street facade had more of the profile of a typical cathedral with its columns and pair of towers, but there was a uniqueness to its overall style, a resplendent enclave of the Polish neighborhood. There was a sense of discovery in coming to this place, and Roger slowly checked the pace of his walk until he stood still on the sidewalk, looking up in thought. It then became apparent to Peaches that this was their destination. "A church? I think we all could use some prayer and preaching after what we've been through, but it's not even Sunday! I didn't know you were that pious."

"Nor am I that Catholic! Nonetheless, I do have some

business here before we get back on the train. I don't expect it should take too long. I'm hoping there's someone here who can help me, otherwise our trip here will be very short indeed. You can either come in with me or perhaps find a priest for confession?"

"How did you know I was Catholic?" Peaches asked, astonished, and perhaps a little embarrassed about the question regarding confession.

"I didn't, but now I do. Otherwise, it's shaping into another fine day even with the lake breeze, so you could get a very nice perspective of the building if you went for a stroll."

"I think I'll just hang out around here, if it's all the same to you. Don't forget about our train."

The interior of the building was conversely austere. Roger entered with reverence, removing his hat, and saw the color spilling into the worship area from the rose window. The main altar was visible and properly adorned, but the side hallways and areas outside of the nave showed signs of incompletion. From where he stood, Roger observed that the interior of the dome lacked a fresco. He speculated that some plasterwork was forthcoming for many of the walls as would a general beatification process before this grand shell of a building would match its exterior grace. It appeared that Saturday morning mass had recently let out, as a few people were still in the nave, perhaps praying the Rosary. Roger searched for a priest, and felt unprepared as he heard what must have been Polish being gently spoken between two parishioners in the narthex nearby. "You . . . I've seen you before!" A familiar voice called out to him in English. The Archbishop Sebastian Messmer was trailed by an attendant, having just come from a side room, perhaps the vestry. "You're that reporter from Chicago. Roger, I believe your name was. Have you come to join the Mother Church?" he asked seriously, reading gloom in the man's expression.

"Archbishop Messmer, Sebastian, uh, no I'm sorry. But I'm very glad to have run into you here. I wonder if you have a few minutes? There is a certain matter I'd like to discuss."

"I have a lunchtime meeting at Mader's uptown," Sebastian said with a smile, clasping a hand on Roger's shoulder. "But I can spare you a spell of my time. There is a little space that I use here. Come! We will have a seat."

Sebastian led Roger down elegantly shaped hallways of stone. Roger remembered the words of Reginald's occult experiences, and his mind was visited by unwelcome imaginings of floating revenants who may haunt such lofty and echoing corridors. Eventually, the two stepped through a door into a side room. They each had a seat, and Sebastian's hand came to idly rest on his pectoral cross, which was underscored by his more modest vestments. The office also had a bit of a spartan feel, although there were some paintings on the wall, one of which was a baroque devotional painting of the Church's namesake, Josaphat. Roger thought he looked very saintly, even Christ-like in the painting. "A great servant of the Lord, he was martyred in the 1600s, an archbishop himself," Sebastian explained as he noticed Roger's upward gaze. "We'll have to get a mural of him, perhaps behind the altar," he sighed. "Another expense, another necessity!"

"Very interesting," Roger said politely, nodding and regarding the portrait. "I see what you mean. It is a breathtaking place," he added, tilting his head up to include the larger space. "And about the work-in-progress being done with the interior."

Sebastian frowned at that. "My heart is with the growth of Catholic education, but even the very bones of this church are such a striking expression of faith . . . it ought to be declared a basilica, to the glory of God, and will be once it's completed. But I cannot tell you how much costs can spiral out of control, even when you start with a straightforward plan! There will be a bit of debt, it's no secret. That topic comes up so much in general councils in the archdiocese, it's as if we had nothing else to discuss. Maybe now that you've seen the situation and the building for yourself, you could let the faithful and generous-in-heart down Chicago know that gifts would be appreciated?" Roger leaned back slightly, surprised by his initiative. "But I'm sorry, you called this meeting, not me," the archbishop resumed. "Please tell me what's on your mind, son. I'm sorry, I'm lapsing into the form of these interminable talks I keep finding myself in lately."

"It's all right! I think I remember when we did an article when the Church was finished and consecrated in 1901. That was my second year at the *Tribune*. In fact, I could see about a piece being done today, through a little editorial, though I would have to convince my editor. You understand, it's a bit tricky navigating that sort of thing. We want to appear neutral-minded, but I could promise a little mention of the situation, at the very least. I wonder if you could provide a small favor for me as well?"

"I'm not sure what spiritual services we could guide you toward, Mr. Merrick. I pray you don't mean financial compensation!"

"No—nothing like that! Let me show you something." Roger opened his jacket, then clumsily reached into his pocket and fumbled for the dagger with his left hand. He carefully unwound the knife's edge that had been wrapped with extra bandage cloth, then placed it on the table in front of the archbishop, who regarded it with wonder and confusion. "I would like a new and permanent home for this. I have a certain reverence for this dagger. It saved my life, and I would like it somewhere safe, but also totally irrecoverable. Perhaps in a nook or vault within . . . this church? In a little insert in the wall as construction continues?" He leaned forward at the stunned clergyman, now even enjoying the moment. "I think the amber coloration is handsome enough to adorn the base of a reliquary chamber."

"Roger, what do you think it is that we do here? I don't claim to be an expert on Lutheranism, but this seems bizarre, even for a Protestant! Where on Earth did you find such a thing?"

"I think it could be very much at home here, where its presence may go unnoticed, and its potency dampened. It's impossibly ancient, yet strong. But mainly, there's something . . .

more to it. Like it has its own sort of energy. I wouldn't call it negative energy, but it's almost intoxicating unto itself, and weighs on and drains the wielder."

"You do know that Milwaukee has a very good public museum?" The archbishop rebuffed, regarding the eccentric journalist more cautiously now. "I daresay you have a good number of them down in Chicago, too!"

"Sebastian, please, *totally irrecoverable*, I had said," Roger stated, trying not to sound demanding. "I must not possess this any longer, but I don't want a scholar's attempt to expound its origins on a little panel right next to it, on display for the world!" Again, Roger had inadvertently raised his voice, and as he removed his hand from his brow, he saw beads of sweat. "What better place to store such a potent thing than a House of God? I can't say why, exactly, but I thought that this would be the place for it," he finished with exasperation.

Sebastian considered the proposition more seriously now, whether out of sympathy or if only to humor and momentarily quell the insistent man. He picked up the keen weapon and examined it, tracing the outline of the hilt, and then the flat of the dagger's edge, carefully with his index finger. A slight change came over his countenance. "You did not mention where you found this thing. It certainly doesn't look European, so it leads one to guess it's a Native craft?" Sebastian sighed and placed the dagger back down on the table, and Roger wondered if the archbishop truly desired a full explanation. The reporter mentally prepared the tale, once again, and breathed deeply. "No, I won't press for the truth," the archbishop explained. "I don't expect it shall set me free in this case, and I do not wish for it to taste like ash in your mouth either. An editorial, then?" he asked, to which Roger nodded, vigorously. "And you can assure me this isn't stolen?"

"I can assure you. In fact, I don't think anyone with any proper claim to it is alive today. I rediscovered it, in a sense."

The archbishop pondered for another moment, then laughed. "In a sense," he echoed Roger. "I suppose you've done all of the work here. I just find somewhere to store this thing— somewhere here," he emphasized, responding to the worried look from Roger at his wording. "And that concludes things. Perhaps the strangest request I ever honor, but I am fond of Ms. Lucy and her Spring House, and I know that she is very fond of you! That's enough for me." He picked up the dagger and placed it in a drawer, locking it with a key that he produced from his pocket. "Until it finds a permanent spot," he again reassured Roger. "I look forward to reading what you have to say regarding our efforts here," he said, rising, shaking Roger's hand. "I'm glad you didn't suggest that I pass it off as some long-forgotten relic. That joke grows thin very swiftly, even among the impious, and I'm not sure how many blessed daggers are mentioned in the hagiographies."

Roger offered his thanks and left the looming building. He had forgotten to wind his pocket watch at the start of the day, but it was still ticking, showing a time of 9:28. A coach had pulled up with its door ajar, and he could see Peaches looking out at him, waving for him to climb aboard. Later, on board the train, Roger and Peaches settled into their seats. "It's strange," Peaches began. "I half expected some thug or creature to intercept us, but thank God, nothing but a quiet morning! How about that, Roger? Our luck is starting to turn around, don't you think?"

"Luck is a funny thing, Peaches. A funny concept. I never really like to think of things in those terms," Roger said quietly, never shifting his gaze away from the window as the train began moving, the southern neighborhood of Milwaukee smoothly passing by. "It's almost a form of fatalism. What do you say for Cynthia Lowell, or even a man like Tom Moss, dying that way? They had bad luck all the way? Their luck ran out? I like to think that our decisions are what guide our own fate. You know, free will and all that? But then you see something like we did, and you feel a coldness. A coldness on a cosmic scale . . . unseen energies and entities that we can nearly say with all certainty . . . that we *should* be ably to say, do not exist. But something drove the life force of that abomination, something lends power to a figure like Reginald Linden. We take solace in our beliefs, and in each other, but what paltry match could these be for such forces?" Roger paused and looked at Peaches. "Yet if we don't, what are we but naked souls laid bare to the grim realities of this world? Of this veiled universe?"

"Well, I like to think that we are living proof that there's some providence afoot, straightening things out! As for solace, I'm a simple man and take it in baseball, beer, and beautiful women," Peaches replied. "Although the latter has a strange habit of not taking solace in me! Promise me you won't screw things up by opening your next conversation with Ms. Lucy like this, will you?"

Roger laughed, and the two of them discussed lighter matters on the two-hour train ride. They also were coming to terms with the fact that soon they would at last part ways, at least for a time. Peaches proposed a resolution to the issue, with his usual boisterous optimism. "We can always grab a drink! We aren't that far away from each other as it turns out! Although a couple miles in Chicago can feel longer than walking through those lonely roads and Waukesha farms."

A trainman came by, announcing that it was five minutes to Union Depot, downtown Chicago. "I sure as hell am looking forward to reading your stories in the paper," Peaches resumed, "maybe even put the money down for a subscription. There's a different feeling to reading it when you've had a hand in making it, after all. Hopefully the next big story you cover will be when the Cubbies win the Series in a little less than a year!"

"Is that a prediction?" Roger asked.

"That cosmic energy you were talking about? I'm channeling it right now, so it's a promise."

For the first time in what felt like ages, Roger walked alone. He carried his tremendously precious stories with as much security as he could muster. He had never carried something so valuable before, a feeling he estimated as some must feel when holding their own child. In the same way the stories were a part of him, he had poured part of himself into them, and he was changed by putting it to paper, nearly to the extent that experiencing the bizarre events firsthand had impacted him. At thirty-one years of age, having neither wife nor child nor knowledge of the reception that his stories would face, Roger suddenly felt both aged and vulnerable. Lou Baker could rag on his stories and take one his fat cigar stubs and burn a hole through the main body of his page, but Roger knew—he had convinced himself—that he would be all right. He had decided that was not where the true value of that manila folder ultimately resided.

The journalist had danced along the line of succumbing to madness and the despair of an indifferent universe since he awoke at the hospital with pain and nightmares. But now he sought to emerge from that malaise as he had from the grotto of Haunchyville. Roger walked under an overcast sky down Michigan Avenue, hoping that the physical and mental wounds would heal in time, and knowing that the scars would be great. Phantom dwarves and sinister shapes offered unease and alarm in the shadows of his peripheral sight. He had become a reluctant adversary to the new-age warlock and incognito warden of midnight-black monsters of the river. On the verge of being affirmed in his career, he now questioned where his path must lead. Entrusted to investigate the arcane mysteries of the universe, Roger's waking thoughts became tinted darker with wonder and fear.

Epilogue: Grim Correspondence

Roger returned home from the *Tribune*. His right hand ached as the air was damp that day. The hand had pronounced scar-tissue and patches of darker skin where his flesh had returned. He could not work without using it daily, however, and rotated through a medley of alcohol and pain medication that kept his routine in a flux between haze or pain. He now owned his own apartment in a newer, nine-story building that was only a five-minute walk from work. The space was still a bit empty, but boasted electric lighting and brand-new radiators. There was even one such unit in the bedroom. He and his wife, Lucy Merrick, had only enjoyed the space for the past two months and were still settling in. The Cubs still had not yet won the World Series, but their prospects were improving. Unfortunately, Peaches had been released from the team after the 1903 season, but this meant that he often would visit with Roger and had not yet given up his hopes of returning to play. It was nearly three years after Roger had undertaken his fateful journey to Waukesha and published the stories that had cemented his reputation as a journalist. He remembered clearly his interaction with Lou when he had presented him with the tidier, typed version of Peaches's draft.

"Before, the best story I had read from the Milwaukee area had to do with beer," Lou Baker had said as he finished reading *Spring City Terror*, hot from the press. "In that article, it said that, 'Two cities have been formed by two loves. Chicago, by the love of hot dogs, Milwaukee, by the love of beer. St. Augustine of Hippo,' he chortled, and congratulated Roger by offering a cigar, which was accepted on this occasion. "But this stuff above windswept fields under waning moonlight, bodies floating in spring pools, shotgun blasts barking in the dark, and a madman chittering about a Haunchyville cut down by swift justice? You've found your breakthrough! Crass name, though . . . Haunchyville. Seems off. Maybe consider modifying that. I wonder how the locals will feel once they get wind of the story?"

As it turned out, despite the considerable upheaval the murders had on the community, the residents of Waukesha didn't object to Roger's stories. Intermittently, he received complimentary mail, as well as updates. St. Josaphat's Church was still in a bit of financial trouble, despite the editorial piece going out, and progress remained slow completing the interior. Roger's stolen article on Haunchyville had appeared in a slightly altered form in a handful of publications in Wisconsin, but the report was far enough from the truth that he decided to leave the matter be. Reginald Linden had apparently deserted his position at Carroll College and was declared officially missing. Roger grimly desired that this owed to Reginald's body rotting away in the Haunchyville grotto; Roger never deigned to return and to confirm this, preferring that Haunchyville remained a memory. Before the auction of the professor's estate, however, there had been a break-in and his study had been pillaged of many of its rare books. The Fountain Spring House did hang on until 1905, beating Lucy's initial estimate by a full year. Then it was finally sold to the Metropolitan Church Association of Chicago, now functioning as a schoolhouse.

Lucy found profession as a typist for the *Tribune* and so far had enjoyed her life with Roger in the Windy City. Some nights, either one or both of them would deal with dark phantoms in their dreams. Shadowy masses lurched through the water, a long-haired, faceless warlock chanted at them in an unknown tongue, waves of heat seemed to burn their very flesh and caused one or both of them wake up in a sweat. For Roger in particular, the haunchymen continually haunted him, and sometimes in his waking moments he espied something odd at the corner of his vision, or when looking up from reading or writing—always for it to be a different shape, or nothing at all. Years after that terrifying October night, impulses of the imagination and subconscious dread had festered far worse than the initial fear that had washed over Roger. When the events had been recent they were almost comprehendable—surviving them was a type of victory. But as with a drenching wave of icy water, the damage was far worse in the shivering aftermath of being unable to regain warmth or dryness. It was their consolation to hold each other through these miserable vigils, wiping the tears from each other's eyes. As they awoke each day, these horrors were momentarily banished by the rising sun, and they took continual comfort in each other's presence, moving forward not just for their own sakes.

Indeed, there was no better companion for either one of them after their shared struggle against the darkness creeping at the brink of their memories. Roger loved Lucy. There was no one more precious to him, yet she often spoke of her desire to bond through happy, ordinary experiences and bring balance to their traumatic connection which still dominated their memory and very relationship. "I want to take joy in trifles and lighter things, like walking through the park and holding your hand, drinking wine together at late parties, going to the theater and laughing. We don't laugh enough . . . I don't expect you to be the same untroubled sentimentalist as you were before all this, but you must try to let it go."

Roger found that laughter came rarely to him, and Lucy could always tell when he was mimicking it. His mood was hamstrung by the constant dull pain in his hand and the persistent thought that it was simply inappropriate to laugh or feel any joy when he had seen a glimpse of the dark side of things. It reminded him of when he had lifted up and examined a large rock as a child and discovered a colony of slugs. The same truth had been conveyed again; one must assume the existence of unseemly things beneath the surface, out of the light. Furthermore, Roger feared that Lucy now begrudged how he acted when Peaches joined them from time to time; the former ballplayer's unflinching absurdity and oblivious immunity to depression had a unique effect in evoking echoes of mirth in Roger. It was not that he was discontent, but his countenance became reserved, and he lacked outward signs of jollity. His good-natured expression was replaced by bags under his eyes from restless nights when the nerves beneath his skin changed to yellowed roots in his dreams. Yet, in a number of quiet moments, Lucy and Roger shared droplets from the vial of that unencumbered happiness from when they first kissed, and there was an unspoken hope that things would progressively improve.

Roger had been no stranger to receiving increased correspondence since his breakthrough stories, but on a late September afternoon, he received a letter that was addressed for him that was sent to the *Tribune* instead of his home address. This had happened on one previous occasion when a certain newly-tenured Professor Henry Armitage, from some East Coast university Roger had never heard of, had written him. Armitage proposed a meeting on his next trip to Chicago to further discuss Roger's story—a date that was fast approaching. This present letter did not bear a return address, however, and Roger took it up to his office before opening it. The handwriting had a certain familiarity, although now had a spidery shakiness to it.

Dear Roger,

I hope that this letter of courtesy finds you well, but neither complacent nor comfortable. You led me through such a humbling experience that my disposition remains inexorably mixed. I learned much from you about my own vulnerabilities, weaknesses, indulgences, blindness. Yet you also caused me considerable trouble in the rendering of this lesson—trouble that I still am reeling from, bodily and spiritually. At the same time, I will credit that you did not seek my death, despite us becoming adversaries. From my limited observation you sought only to preserve your own life in the face of the peril of the aberrant dark young. I will not attribute that to you as mercy. In fact, it is a form of neutrality. I am trying to transcend my emotions and therefore inform you of my subsequent neutrality. I will not actively seek you, and you may pray that our paths never cross again if you are so foolishly inclined to search for me. My primal instincts born of Thalmak's succor grow as I attempt to suppress them, and I wager I would send you and your pretty Lucy to a scorching hell were you to meet my sight again. I will strengthen my appeals to Rooted Whisperer beneath the Earth and risk even the wrath of Abhoth in my chthonic search for Thalmak's vault, unto the fruition of his hour. For all of its shortcomings, let us commend the utility of the Post Office Department in allowing me to convey this message, which I do not deny has led to some satisfaction on my part!

Yours,

Reginald Wingate Linden

Roger sweat, and his hands trembled as he set down the letter. He had quietly kept the possibility of Reginald's survival to a near impossibility for these years. Trying to convince himself of its unlikeliness, he nonetheless had not forgotten the moment that he fled the grotto with Reginald's fate left uncertain. Now, after Roger had received his letter, he found that he had not been surprised by it. In one sense it brought relief; he no longer had to speculate or be plagued by incessant wondering. On the other hand, the words left him deeply shaken as again he heard their sharp narration of Reginald's voice in his head. Since Roger's return to Chicago, each day had felt a degree brighter, as the dark hue of his past gradually receded from him. But this piece of paper effected a profound reversal. Reginald Linden and his imposed reality would never be displaced from Roger's conscious thoughts so long as he lived; if Roger did not act in the wake of this, it would be to concede the very concepts of sanity and goodness. The professor had proclaimed the redoubling of his efforts in contacting greater and, perhaps, additional shrouded entities after losing his dominion of a lesser horror. In the same way he grew tired of the Astral Yeoman, Reginald had graduated to a school of greater madness. Roger, too, would intensify his activities, and he had not been idle by any means.

Roger got out of his chair and stood to look out of the window overlooking Dearborn Street. There was so much activity: stacked foodstuffs on truck beds, newspapers, industry, all floating by in a dizzying scramble. It seemed like there were always a few more people crowding the walks each day. The world continued to progress and shrink, yet it was of no help to his private torments. He could not decide if he preferred his nemesis as a distant abstraction or a foe at the threshold, ready to do deadly combat. The pull of grim focus and new energy had arrived with this taunting declaration. Roger would not let himself be cowed.

Roger had cut a hole in the fence called reality and lacked the means to repair it and return within. He crossed over to his desk, opening the locked drawer at the bottom, and retrieved a decrepit book, placing it very delicately on the desktop. It had been sent to him by Sam River in a parcel with no message some time ago, who Roger suspected had pilfered it from Reginald's collection. Whether or not Sam had been responsible for the sloppier and large-scale break-in to steal the other books, Roger never pressed. Yet, as always, when he opened the strange grimoire and began his ponderous progress of decipherment, he felt a surge of energy, of resolution, the means to combat, to overcome such skulking figures like Reginald Linden. The activity was a close secret; Roger had decided this burden must be his alone. He had given the book a name from a character that often recurred in the rambling pages: *X'arta's Book of Remedy* titled his notes. Roger was making progress, and he learned of the recitations of Thalmak, Yog-Sothoth, and other mad appellations that appeared in the voluminous pages. The potent miasma of decadent rumination lifted off of the very pages whenever the book was opened. Roger was a wanderer, still a self-avowed novice in the shrill darkness. He would continue his stumbling to discover a light, or until his eyes adjusted to the crepuscule.

Sean Michael Malone is a native and lifelong resident of Southeastern Wisconsin. Sean earned his B.A. in European History from Concordia University Wisconsin and his M.A. in Medieval History from Marquette University. He enjoys finding inspiration in travelling with his wife, Athena, especially observing the natural beauty of New Zealand's Fiordland and reflecting in the shadow of historical sites of France, the United Kingdom, and Ireland. He currently resides in West Allis, Wisconsin.